MIDDLE SCHOOL

SCHOOL

BORN TO ROCK

JAMES PATTERSON

AND CHRIS TEBBETTS

ILLUSTRATED BY NEIL SWAAB

1 3 5 7 9 10 8 6 4 2

Young Arrow
20 Vauxhall Bridge Road
London SW1V 2SA

Young Arrow is part of the Penguin Random House group of companies
whose addresses can be found at global.penguinrandomhouse.com

Penguin
Random House
UK

First published in Great Britain by Young Arrow in 2019
This edition published in paperback by Young Arrow in 2020

www.penguin.co.uk

A CIP catalogue record for this book
is available from the British Library

ISBN 9781784753962

Printed and bound in Great Britain by Clays Ltd, Elcograf S.p.A.

Penguin Random House is committed to a sustainable future
for our business, our readers and our planet. This book is made
from Forest Stewardship Council® certified paper.

MIDDLE SCHOOL
BORN TO ROCK

My Name is Georgia Khatchadorian (But You Probably Already Knew That, Didn't You?)

I've wanted to be a famous rock star for a long time now. Then the other day I got my wish.

Believe it or not, I'm famous now. *Everyone* in my hometown knows who I am. In fact, it feels like everywhere you look these days—*there I am again*.

Just not in a good way.

More like a ruin-your-life, wish-you-could-crawl-in-a-hole-and-never-come-out kind of way.

And if you know anything about me and my family, then you won't be surprised when I tell you this is all my big brother Rafe's fault.

Have you ever heard the story of King Midas? He's the guy who turned everything into piles of gold just by touching it. Well, my brother is like the opposite of that. Everything *he* touches turns into huge, enormous piles of *disaster*.

Who, me?

Like, for instance, my life.

For the record, I'm not saying I'm perfect. I've made plenty of mistakes along the way, and I've had some *Titanic*-sized disasters of my very own. But none of it erases the fact that trouble follows my brother around the same way that an awful smell follows a skunk everywhere it goes.

Don't worry, I'm going to tell you all about it. But to do that, I really need to take a step back and start this story where every story starts. At the beginning.

And this one begins with a single, solitary egg.

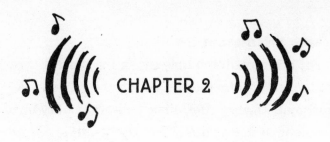

CHAPTER 2

The Challenge

The name of the assignment was the Great Egg Drop Challenge. Our science teacher, Mrs. Hibbs, said that everyone had to design a capsule that would protect an ordinary egg from breaking when it got thrown off the roof of Hills Village Middle School.

Kind of cool, right?

For my capsule, I used a shoebox. Inside it I put a block of Styrofoam with an egg-sized hole cut out, and I tied five purple helium balloons to the outside.

Those balloons were my secret weapon. If this worked, my capsule was going to float gently down to the ground like it was made of feathers. I was

really careful about the
way I designed the whole
thing and spent a lot of time
putting it together for a few
days before it was due.

As for my brother, I
think he started his project
about ten minutes before
we had to leave for school
that morning. I could hear
him crashing around in his room while I ate my
pancakes.

"What's he doing in there?" Grandma Dotty
asked.

"Just barely scraping by," I said, because it's
true. The last time Rafe got his homework done
ahead of time was…never.

"Rafe! If you want me to drive you to school,
now's the time!" Mom yelled.

"Here I come!" he said, which is when his project
came rolling down the hall.

Have you ever seen *Raiders of the Lost Ark*?
You know that part where a giant boulder goes
tumbling after Indiana Jones and it's so big it

takes up the whole tunnel? Well, that's about what our hallway looked like just then. Except instead of a boulder, it was a giant ball made out of Bubble Wrap. Miles and miles and miles of Bubble Wrap.

"That's your egg capsule?" I said.

"When in doubt, think big!" Rafe said.

Basically, that's my brother's motto. But he also has a history of BIG-thinking his way into BIG trouble. Which is why my motto is more like, "When in doubt, do the opposite of Rafe."

"It's not even going to fit in the car," Mom said.

"That's what this is for," Rafe said, holding up some rope. "It's going on the roof."

I couldn't tell if Rafe's capsule was going to pass the challenge or if his egg would wind up like Humpty Dumpty Junior on the sidewalk. And to be honest, I didn't really care. I just wanted to get an A on my own project.

IMPORTANT FACT #1: There are some things you're going to need to know for this story. The first is that Rafe and I are in some of the same classes, even though I'm younger than him. Mom says we all have our own special talents. Being smart wasn't one of Rafe's.

But you know what else? If I'd known about the Mount Everest–sized trouble that egg was going to cause by the end of the day, I would have faked sick, stayed home, and skipped the whole thing. Too bad for me—I'm better at science than I am at seeing into the future.

So I got in the car with Mom and Rafe and headed off to school to begin the craziest, best-worst, most up-down and awful (but also awesome…but mostly awful) day of my life.

So far.

CHAPTER 3

Sam and Eggs (Get It?)

Here we go!" Mrs. Hibbs yelled from the roof of the gym. "Let the Great Egg Drop Challenge begin!"

And just like that, it started raining egg capsules.

Mrs. Hibbs sure knows how to make science class fun. She's one of my favorite teachers because of her awesome project assignments. And it was especially fun to see my own capsule touch down at about zero miles an hour. And let's just say, some of the landings weren't as graceful as mine was. I wouldn't be exaggerating if I said it honestly looked like some capsules exploded on contact.

I held my breath the whole time it took me to retrieve my shoebox, but when I looked inside, my egg was still whole, not a gloppy mess. Yes!

Mine wasn't the only one, either. About half of the eggs made it through the challenge, including Rafe's. His giant Bubble Wrap ball got the most attention when it dropped and bounced a few times, but it definitely wasn't the best capsule. The best one was Sam Marks's. He made a whole self-deploying parachute for his, which was a bit like my balloon idea, but better. And more sophisticated. And cooler.

Which brings me to…

IMPORTANT FACT #2: I have a big fat crush on Sam Marks.

Sam is the cutest boy I've ever known. He's also really nice. Nice to be around. Nice to look at. Nice to everyone he knows, including me. And it doesn't even seem like he's pretending!

We even danced at a school dance one time, but I didn't know if that meant Sam liked me the way I liked him…or not.

That's the problem with *nice*. It can mean all kinds of things!

So anyway, I was putting my capsule away after class, and Sam came right up to me at my locker.

"Hey, Georgia," he said. "Cool capsule."

"Thanks!" I said. "But yours was better. My balloons will only last for—"

"Twelve to twenty hours," he said. "I know. I thought about using them, but then I came up with the parachute instead."

I haven't even mentioned yet how smart Sam is. He's kind of a geek, but that's one of the reasons I like him. I'm kind of a geek, too. Which makes us perfect for each other. Sam probably just hasn't realized it yet.

I didn't get any closer to finding out, either. Because that's when the first really bad thing happened that day. And it was really, *really* bad— almost as if a dark, evil shadow that brought pain and suffering to everything it touched just happened to cross my path at the exact wrong moment.

And this time, I'm not even talking about Rafe.

BEWARE ALL WHO TURN THIS PAGE!

CHAPTER 4

Princesses on Patrol

That's when Missy Trillin came slithering by.

At school, Missy is the Queen of Mean. The Duchess of Darkness. The Sultan of Snobbery.

Missy makes it her full-time business to make sure everyone knows how much better she is.

"Oh, look who it is," she said. "Tell me, you two. Which came first? The geek or the egg?"

Which is when her two friends started cackling like they were at a junior witch convention. I call them the "Princess Patrol," because the princesses keep changing so there's no point in using their names. These days, Alicia and Chloe are on patrol, but Missy Trillin switches best friends the way other people change their underwear.

The thing about the Princesses is, you can't avoid them. They're just an unfortunate fact of life. Like diseases. Or tornadoes. Or that boiled vegetable medley they serve in the cafeteria.

Boy, do I hate that vegetable medley. It's like Alicia and Chloe are the mushy carrots and corn and Missy is the lima beans, which are twice as bad as both of the other two put together.

Before Sam could answer Missy's mean little joke, I glared right at her. "Buzz off, Lima Bean," I said. "We're talking here."

"Did you just call me Lima Bean?" Missy said.

The other two looked at me like I'd spat on the Queen of England. Or, at least, the Queen of Hills Village Middle School. Nobody talks to Missy that way, but I gave up worrying about her a long time ago.

Still, I probably shouldn't have made that "buzz off" comment. And I don't mean because it was rude or uncalled-for—I mean, I shouldn't have said it the same way you shouldn't poke a hornet's nest with a stick.

So there I was, standing between the nicest boy at HVMS and the meanest, most vile collection of girls on the face of the earth, not knowing what to do next, when something else came along and changed everything...*again*. I told you this was a roller-coastery kind of day, right?

Because that's when the world's coolest news hit like a ray of sunshine made out of hundred-dollar bills and unlimited Skittles.

But you're just going to have to turn the page again to find out what I mean.

I WARNED YOU <u>NOT</u> TO TURN THE PAGE! TWICE!

CHAPTER 5

Best. News. Ever!

Before Missy could pounce, and before Sam could say another word, my friends Nanci, Mari, and Patti came running up the hall, grabbed me by the arm, and just kept on moving, sweeping me right along with them.

"Come with us," Mari said.

"What's going on?" I said.

"Something good," Patti said. "See you later, Sam! Georgia has to go now!"

They totally ignored the Princesses. But as we were flying away, I heard Chloe behind me.

"Why did Georgia call you Lima Bean?" she asked.

"Shut up, Chloe," Missy said.

"See you later, Georgia!" Sam called, and just like that I was gone with the wind. I mean, with the band.

IMPORTANT FACT #3: I'm in a band. Like an actual, real band. That's a big part of this story, too. It's pretty cool, but probably not as cool as it sounds. For starters, the band's name is We Stink.

Obviously, this had something to do with We Stink—but what? Whatever it was, it had to be some kind of high-security matter, because we headed straight for the bathroom. And believe me, nobody goes in there for the cozy atmosphere.

"Look at THIS!" Nanci said, as soon as the door swung shut behind us. She held up her phone and pressed Play on a video of a commercial.

"Why are you—?" I said.

"Just listen!" Mari said.

The voice in the ad said: "Okay, all you young rock stars and mock stars out there, start warming up, because Lulu and the Handbags are looking for a warm-up act."

I'm not sure what it said next, because I was too busy screaming. It was like my ears blew open, my brain caught on fire, and my stomach filled up with popping corn, all at the same time.

Lulu and the Handbags is one of my three favorite bands, and Lulu is my number one idol. She's totally cool, and talented, and she's not a supermodel or a princess or any of those other things. She's just Lulu.

And Lulu is AWESOME.

"It's open to anyone under sixteen," Nanci said. "First, you have to post a video on the contest site. Then the top twelve vote-getters will be invited to the live auditions. And the winner of that round will be the warm-up act for Lulu's big show in the city—"

"*And* win a thousand bucks!" Mari said, and we all screamed again.

To be honest, I don't like all that girly stuff, like screaming when you're excited. But for Lulu, I made an exception. If anything was worth screaming over, I'd say that a chance to meet my idol and warm up for her band was it.

This was turning out to be the best day ever!

For about another twenty seconds.

CHAPTER 6

Caught in the Act

I was just about to start watching that ad on Nanci's phone again when the bathroom door swung open.

Our principal, Mrs. Stricker, was standing right there looking at us like she'd snared four little chipmunks in her trap.

"Section three, rule two, from the Hills Village Middle School code of conduct!" Her voice echoed off the slightly slimy tiled walls. "No unauthorized cell phone usage is allowed in school except for emergencies!"

I broke in, "But Mrs. Stricker—"

"Is this an emergency?" she said.

Patti tried to get a word in. "Well—"

"No, it is not," Mrs. Stricker said. "Was there any reasonable cause for all the screaming?"

"Kind of," I said.

"No, there was not," Mrs. Stricker said.

"Are those *detention* slips?" I asked, once I saw the little pink pieces of paper in her hand.

"Yes, they are," Mrs. Stricker said. "Unless someone's hair is on fire or a wild animal has been set loose in the halls, there is *never* any reason for that kind of screaming in my school. Not to mention the cell phone."

Believe me, I know what a detention slip looks like, and it's not because I've had so many of them. It's because Rafe could wallpaper our whole apartment with the ones he's gotten.

I couldn't even argue with Mrs. Stricker. The fact was, we *had* broken the rules. Mom wasn't going to be too happy about this, either.

Rafe, on the other hand? He'd probably be proud of me.

As we came out of the bathroom, Missy and her

regal court of butt-kissers were standing right there, watching us.

"Oh, was that you in there?" Missy asked. "I thought it was a bunch of stray cats dying. So I thought I should report it to Mrs. Stricker. *Sorrr-eee!*"

"I knew it was them," Chloe said. "But I thought all that screaming was their 'band practice.'"

"How can you tell the difference?" Alicia said. "They stink!"

"It's *We* Stink," Nanci said.

"Same thing," Missy said, and the other two cracked up like Missy would immediately dump them if they didn't laugh their heads off.

I could still hear them laughing as Mrs. Stricker marched us toward the office. And all I could think about was sticking the Princess Patrol into a giant egg capsule, attaching it to a weather balloon, and sending the whole thing out over the Pacific Ocean.

Hopefully never to be seen again.

CHAPTER 7

The Detention Song

ONE NIGHT ONLY!

Lulu AND THE HANDBAGS

WITH Special Guest

WE STINK!

A Walking Disaster

As soon as detention was over, the girls and I agreed to race home, get our stuff, and meet at the We Stink studio. Which is really just my garage.

The deadline for contest entries was coming up fast. We had to pick a song, make our video, and get it online, ASAHP (as soon as humanly possible).

So I definitely had a lot on my mind. I also had a lot in my hands, including my backpack, my lunch bag, and my egg capsule, with the egg still inside.

All of which means I wasn't paying attention to where I was going as I hurried home.

IMPORTANT FACT #4: For me, hurrying is a

little slower than it is for some people. My left leg is two centimeters shorter than my right leg. When I'm standing around with bare feet, I call myself the Leaning Tower of Georgia. I have to wear special shoes to make up the difference. My doctor says I'll probably outgrow it by the time I'm an adult. But in the meantime, I limp a little bit when I walk.

Also, my head was so full of fantasies about meeting Lulu and the Handbags, I didn't notice that I'd taken the "dangerous" way home until it was too late. And that meant I went right past the Trillin estate.

Yes, *estate.*

I'm not going to lie. Missy's family has the nicest house in Hills Village by a mile. It's surrounded by big, high gated walls, and out front there's a big statue of Major Zachary Hills. He's the founder of our town (we named it after him!), and also Missy's great-great-great-great-grandfather. Of course.

"Nice walk!" somebody yelled out.

I looked up, and it was Missy with her dog, Benjamins, coming down the driveway and out through their gate.

"Do you use that strut on the runways in Paris?" Missy asked.

And I thought, *seriously?* This girl had everything you could possibly want from the catalog of life, and she still had to make fun of the way I walked?

I know it shouldn't have hurt my feelings, because Missy is an evil troll. It doesn't seem fair that someone who doesn't have any feelings can hurt yours. But it did.

And that's probably why I snapped.

Before I knew what I was doing, I popped open that capsule of mine. I reached in. I took out my egg. And I winged it right at Missy—and made a direct hit.

"You IDIOT!" Missy screamed. "Do you know how much this T-shirt cost?"

I'm not normally the type to throw eggs at people. Even at evil people. That's more of a Rafe move than a Georgia move. But now I was going to pay a Rafe-sized price, because Missy was letting her giant Doberman off the leash and pointing him my way.

"Sic 'er, Benjamins! Eat the geek!" she said.

I may be a little slow, but I'm not bad at

climbing. So I went for the nearest high thing I could, which was the wall around the Trillin estate. It's all covered in ivy, and just like that, I was heading straight up before Benjamins could find out what I tasted like.

I also kept looking back. That was another mistake. Because at the top of the wall, there was a big concrete planter. It was the kind of thing you might look at and think, "I sure hope nobody ever bumps into that and knocks it off the wall." You might not even guess someone my size could be strong enough to do that.

But you'd be wrong.

"Watch it!" Missy screamed, just before I plowed into that planter...

...and just before it tipped right off the wall...

...and landed on top of Major Hills's statue...

...*and knocked his head clean off.*

I had just decapitated Major Hills, the village hero. Also known as Missy's great-great-great-great-grandfather. And now his head was rolling to a stop in the Trillins' driveway.

Something told me I wasn't going to make it to band practice on time.

CHAPTER 9

Head Honcho

I'd always been curious about what the inside of the Trillins' mansion looked like. But this sure wasn't the way I wanted to find out.

When Mom showed up, I was sitting there, drinking water with a lemon slice in it, like I'd been booked into the world's nicest prison.

I felt awful. I hated making trouble for Mom, just as much as I hated the way Missy kept glaring at me. You would have thought I'd declared war on all of Hills Village, starting with her family.

So when Mrs. Trillin told Mom they weren't going to make me pay for putting Major Hills's head back on, I almost wanted to kiss her. (Mrs. Trillin, I mean. *NOT* Missy.)

"Well, that's very generous," Mom said. "But I do feel as though Georgia should contribute somehow."

And that's when Missy smiled for the first time. Which made ice cubes run through my veins. Believe me, I know what makes Missy Trillin smile, and it has nothing to do with rainbows and puppy dogs.

"I have an idea," Missy said.

And I thought—

No, no, no, no, no...

"Georgia could work here until she's paid off her share," Missy said. And I thought—

No, no, no, no, no, no, no, no!

"Like as a personal assistant. I mean, *Mommy's* assistant, of course. Not mine," Missy said.

ARE YOU KIDDING ME????

I could think of a zillion things that sounded

better than this. In fact, the list was infinite, because there was *nothing* I wanted less than a prison sentence at the Trillins'.

"Well, I *could* use some help around the house a few days a week," Mrs. Trillin said.

I tried to speak up. "I don't know if that's such a good idea—"

"Excuse me?" Mom said to me, staring like I was in no position to complain. Which I wasn't. Whatever happened out there at the gate, I was the one who'd turned Major Hills into the headless non-horseman. Also, that fresh egg on Missy's shirt didn't exactly help my case.

And now Mrs. Trillin was offering us the biggest discount on statue heads anyone had ever seen.

In other words, I didn't have a choice. And just like that, I was the newest member of the Trillin estate staff.

Which also meant working for Missy.

It was like the end of the world. Only worse.

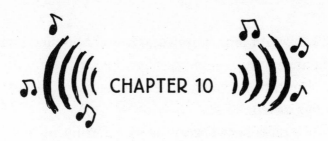

CHAPTER 10

Tick-Tick-Tick

Meanwhile...tick-tick-tick...the contest deadline was coming faster than mold on Rafe's dirty gym socks.

When the band finally got together the next day, we had less than an hour to make our video and get it online. So we just propped Nanci's phone against a paint can in the garage, turned on the camera, and stood there playing our best song. It's called "Let's Shake on It." I wrote the words and Nanci wrote the music. Hopefully it was a Lulu-worthy song, even if it was a lame video.

Either way, we got it posted to the contest site

at 4:56, with four minutes to spare. And now came the hard part.

"How are we going to get people to vote for us?" Nanci asked.

"We have to tell *everyone* we know about this," Patti said.

"It's going to take more than that," I said. "We should keep making videos, and posting pictures of the band wherever we can, with links to the voting page—"

"Who's going to see all that? We don't have any followers," Mari said.

"Then we need to get some!" I said.

"How do we do that?" Nanci asked.

"By putting up videos and pictures and…oh, wait," Mari said.

I guess that's what you call a vicious circle. How were we supposed to get people to vote for us when we didn't have any people?

"What if we played a whole bunch of shows?" I said.

"I like that," Nanci said.

"Ooh!" Mari said. "We could play free bagel Sunday at my dad's used car lot!"

"Do a lot of people come to that?" Patti asked.

"Well…no," Mari said. "But the bagels are really good."

"Maybe we could play at school," Nanci said. "Like at a pep rally or something."

"Except—" Patti looked away.

"Oh, right," Nanci said.

"Mrs. Stricker," we all said at the same time. We weren't exactly on Mrs. Stricker's best side that week. More like her worst side.

"You know what your problem is? You're not thinking big enough," one of the girls said. "Not nearly big enough."

Except, it didn't *sound* like a girl. It sounded like a boy. In fact, it sounded a whole lot like—

"Rafe!" I said. There he was, darkening my studio door. "This is a closed rehearsal. Get out!"

"I was just taking out the trash, but I couldn't help overhearing. It's like your ideas are so bad, they're hurting my ears."

"Goodbye!" I picked up my guitar. "You were just leaving."

"You shouldn't think about getting *votes*," Rafe blabbed on.

"We shouldn't?" Patti looked at him with her head cocked to the side.

"No. You should think about getting *famous*. Then the votes will take care of themselves. If you're going to do this, you might as well do it right."

But I wasn't going to listen to someone with his own permanent chair in the detention room tell me about right and wrong. Especially when that someone was Rafe.

"ONE! TWO! ONE-TWO-THREE-FOUR!" I shouted, and we started jamming out instead. I knew that would get rid of him. And it did.

"You'll be back!" Rafe yelled, even though *he* was the one running for the door. I didn't even know what he meant by that.

At least, not until later, when I figured it out the hard way.

CHAPTER 11

Partners!

The next day, Mrs. Hibbs announced the new project for science.

"Does anyone know what a Rube Goldberg machine is?" she asked. We all shook our heads no, so she showed us some amazing videos.

Rube Goldberg machines usually complete a single, simple job, like turning on a light switch or opening the front door of the house or heating up a frozen pizza, but in a really crazy, complex way.

Say, for instance, you wanted to hand in your homework with a little flair.

2)...Which drops anvil...

5)...Into needle that pops it...

1) Candle burns rope...

3)...Launching cat...

4)...Into toy car, which pushes balloon...

6)...Dropping homework onto desk.

They're made from all kinds of different stuff, and you can use whatever you can find around the house, or in the garage, or at the junk heap. They teach you about physics and engineering and creativity.

I already liked the whole idea of this assignment. And then it got even better.

"All right, everyone," Mrs. Hibbs said. "You'll be working in pairs on your machines. So please pick out a partner and get those brains storming!"

And guess who came straight over to me? Hello, Sam! Hello, *awesome!*

"Georgia, do you want to work on this together?" he asked.

"Sure!" I said. "That would be great."

"Cool," he said. "Because I really like—"

"I like you, too!"

"—what you did with the egg challenge."

"Oh."

I'm surprised I didn't set off the smoke alarm, because it felt like my face was on fire. Even Sam turned red.

Remember when I said how nice it would be if I could see into the future? Well, that goes double for time travel. Because I would have given anything to get a little ten-second do-over just then.

Lucky for me, Sam was extra-nice about it. He just pretended nothing had happened and kept going.

"Do you want to work on it after school?" he asked.

"Sure!" But then I remembered that I had to report to the Trillin estate at four sharp.

"Oh, wait. I can't. I have to, um…babysit, my, uh…brother."

Rafe was a few feet away, sitting there with his head upside down, trying to see something under his desk. Typical.

"Your *older* brother?" Sam asked.

"I'm not supposed to talk about it," I whispered.

I couldn't help myself. Even a crazy lie was better than admitting to Sam that Missy Trillin was my new boss.

"How about first thing next week?" Sam asked.

"That works!" I said.

"Right after school on Monday?" he said.

It was turning back to awesome, all over again. Except then I said, "Sounds like a date!"

Which is, trust me, *not* what you want to say to a boy right after you'd accidentally told him, "I LIKE YOU, TOO!" It was just like getting a do-over after all, because *now* I was just as embarrassed as I had been ten seconds earlier—if not *more* embarrassed.

But as he stood there smiling at me and I stood there smiling at him, I started to wonder if I shouldn't feel *completely* sorry for myself. Even though I probably set a world record for blushing that day, I thought that maybe Sam wasn't being nice just for the sake of being nice. And maybe he wasn't just looking for a science partner, either.

Maybe, I thought...just MAYBE...Sam Marks was starting to like me the same way I liked him. And with any luck, this new assignment was going to give me a chance to find out.

That is, if I didn't embarrass myself to death in the meantime.

First Day, Worst Day

When I rang the Trillins' doorbell that afternoon, I had one thing on my mind: HOW CAN I GET OUT OF THIS?

The short answer was: I couldn't. Not for now, anyway. The deal was for two days a week, 4:00 to 5:30, for the rest of the school year.

Still, I was going to keep my eyes, ears, and brain peeled for any possible exit strategy. Because this was 100 percent the worst thing that had ever happened to me in middle school.

And it hadn't even started yet.

"Georgia! Right on time!" Mrs. Trillin said when

she answered the door. "Come on in, I'll show you around."

She took me down a long hall, then through the enormous shiny kitchen that would've made my mom drool, a family room with at least four couches, another hall, out some French doors, and across the yard. Along the way, I saw maids in pink uniforms, a cook in a white uniform, and a couple of gardeners in green coveralls.

What I *didn't* see, thank goodness, was any sign of Missy. I'd kind of expected her to pounce the second I showed up.

Finally, we came around the corner to the swimming pool, where there was a whole other house that looked about as big as our apartment.

"Have you ever vacuumed a pool before?" Mrs. Trillin asked me.

I looked at the long pole and hose thingy she was holding out for me to take.

"Is it like vacuuming a rug?" I asked.

"Not exactly."

That pool was HUGE. Something told me I was going to be vacuuming it for the rest of the school year. But as long as I was outside and away from the Missy Danger Zone, it could have been worse.

After Mrs. Trillin showed me what to do, she handed me a little walkie-talkie with a headset. She called it a "house radio," because I guess you need that kind of thing when your property is big enough to cross state lines.

"Channel one is Nicole in the kitchen, channel two is Bobby, our head groundskeeper, and I'm on channel three," Mrs. Trillin said. "Just give a shout if you have any questions."

Then she said, "I'll leave you to it"—and disappeared back into the house.

It wasn't so bad at first. All I had to do was run the vacuum across the bottom of the pool, back and forth…and back and forth…

…and back and forth…

Before long, I was a million miles away, thinking about some day in the not-too-distant future when I'd be cleaning my *own* giant swimming pool. Because that's just the kind of internationally famous rock star I'll be. The kind who likes to keep it real.

So when Lulu and the Handbags fly in for a jam session at the studio (the one I'm going to build behind the pool house), I'll want to make sure everything is just right for them.

I mean, maybe it will be a little awkward after I beat Lulu out at the Grammys that year, but we'll work it out. Lulu's cool that way. She'll see my potential, and next thing you know, we'll be back at the Grammys together, performing our mega-smash duet, "Pool Girls."

Then Lulu will score another number one hit of her own. Then I'll score another number one hit. Then Lulu. Then Georgia. Back and forth...

...and back and forth...

…and back and forth…

…and there I was, still cleaning the Trillins' pool. It was all just a nice little dream bubble while I passed the time.

And you know how it is with bubbles, right? They never last long enough.

Because this one was about to go *POP* in a major way.

CHAPTER 13

Pool Girl

The first thing I heard was the sound of the pool house door opening. When I looked over, Missy's Doberman, Benjamins, came running out.

Straight at me.

I dropped my giant vacuum stick (which was a mistake, since it was the closest thing I had to a weapon) and turned to head for the main house.

Too late. He'd already caught up with me. I felt two paws on my shoulders.

"Help!" I yelled.

Benjamins knocked me down, right onto a fluffy pool chaise cushion. I tensed, waiting for those giant Doberman teeth to sink into me.

"HELLLLLP!" I tried again—just before I got a big wet lick on my cheek. And then another lick. And a third slurp that went right in my ear. I couldn't move, but only because Benjamins was giving me doggy kisses like my head was one big ice cream cone.

"Benjamins, COME!" someone said, and he jumped down.

When I looked over, you-know-who was standing there in the pool house door. The Empress of Evil herself.

"Ohhh, *sorrrr-eeee,*" Missy said. "I didn't know you were out here."

In other words, she *definitely* knew I was out there. And she'd been bluffing with Benjamins, too. Because he was no attack dog. He was just a big, scary-looking cream puff.

"Anyway," Missy said. "We're having a little study party in here, and I'm going to need you to take our snack orders."

That's when I realized how many people were inside the pool house. It wasn't just the Princess Patrol. It was more like the Princess Patrol and their whole Popular Posse, all looking at me like I was yesterday's kitchen scraps.

And today's maid.

"Your mom said I should clean the pool," I said,
but Missy snatched my house radio away, turned it
to channel three, and started talking.

"This is Sparkle Sparrow calling Big Bird," she
said. "Mom? Come in, Mom."

The radio squawked and then I heard Mrs. Trillin.

"What is it, sweetheart?" she said. *"I'm in the
middle of a pedicure—"*

"Can I borrow Georgia?" Missy said. "The pool
cleaning can wait, right?"

"Yes, yes, fine," Mrs. Trillin radioed back. *"But for
goodness' sake, Missy, be nice!"*

"Of *coouuurse,*" Missy said, looking at me like
her definition of "nice" was the same as "evil."

Then she gave me back the radio.

"I'll have a blueberry-banana smoothie with
skim milk and vanilla yogurt," Missy told me.

"Me, too," said Chloe, who had marched up
behind her. "But I'm dairy-free. Soy milk for me."

"Can I get strawberry-banana but no yogurt?"
Alicia asked.

"Do you have any chips?" Dexter McCourt asked.
"And maybe some Zoom?"

"You know what? You'd better write this down," Missy said. "Here. You can use the back of this."

She handed me a piece of lavender stationery with some kind of long list on it. I saw lots of words like "clean" and "organize" and "perfect."

"That's my to-do list," Missy said. "Well, more like *your* to-do list now. Don't worry if you can't get to it all today. There's always the next time. Or the time after that."

The whole thing made me want to vomit in Missy's enormous pool. Except of course then I'd just have to clean that up, too.

I also wanted to cry a little. But there was no way I'd let Missy and her Popular Posse see me doing that.

Still, I didn't know what to say. If I told Missy to shove it, would she complain to her mother? And would Mrs. Trillin fire me? And would I be paying for Major Hills's head until I was eighty years old?

I really wasn't sure. Which meant I couldn't risk it.

"Oh, and one other thing," Missy said. Then Alicia came out of the pool house carrying a pink uniform on a hanger. "Make sure you put this

on before you come back with our snacks. 'Kay?
Thaaaaanks."

And that's when I started to realize just how
bad this whole thing was getting.

SQUAWK...Prisoner Khatchadorian, please report to the silver-polishing pavilion!

SQUAWK! We need someone to count the blades of grass on the croquet court!

SQUAWK! Georgia, where ARE you? My toenails aren't gonna paint themselves, you know!

SQUAWK! Cleanup in the third floor southwest bathroom, STAT!

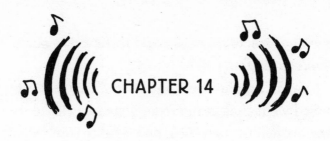

CHAPTER 14

Lemon Bars

I tried talking to Mom about the Missy situation that night, but there wasn't much she could do. It's not like we could suddenly afford to pay for Major Hills's head.

"You know what I'd do?" Mom said. "I'd try to focus on the positive."

"What do you mean? Like how lucky I am that Missy isn't a twin? Or how nice it is to get all that exercise running laps around the Trillin estate?"

"Nothing like that," Mom said. "You're a Khatchadorian, Georgia. We don't always have it easy in life, but we don't give up, either. Try to worry less about Missy and think more about what's been going right lately."

I couldn't argue with that, even if I kind of wanted to. So I went back to my room instead. I closed the door, opened my notebook, and tried to think about something positive. Something good in my life.

Like Lulu.

And the contest.

And We Stink's first number one hit—even if I hadn't written it yet.

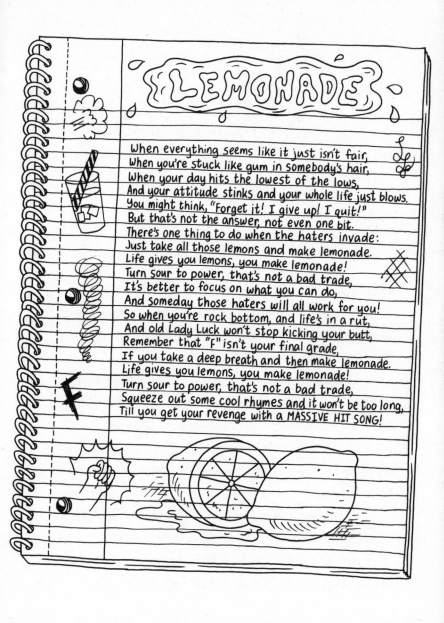

LEMONADE

When everything seems like it just isn't fair,
When you're stuck like gum in somebody's hair,
When your day hits the lowest of the lows,
And your attitude stinks and your whole life just blows.
You might think, "Forget it! I give up! I quit!"
But that's not the answer, not even one bit.
There's one thing to do when the haters invade:
Just take all those lemons and make lemonade.
Life gives you lemons, you make lemonade!
Turn sour to power, that's not a bad trade,
It's better to focus on what you can do,
And someday those haters will all work for you!
So when you're rock bottom, and life's in a rut,
And old Lady Luck won't stop kicking your butt,
Remember that "F" isn't your final grade,
If you take a deep breath and then make lemonade.
Life gives you lemons, you make lemonade!
Turn sour to power, that's not a bad trade,
Squeeze out some cool rhymes and it won't be too long,
Till you get your revenge with a MASSIVE HIT SONG!

Our Big, Medium-Sized Break

Saturday morning, I was outside when I saw our neighbor Mrs. Gorman putting some balloons on her mailbox. There was a HAPPY BIRTHDAY sign on the front door, too.

And that's when it hit me—BRAINSTORM!

McCasalin Gorman was the closest thing our band had to a fan. She came over to the garage sometimes to watch us practice. Probably because she was in the fifth grade, which made us at least a little bit cool to her.

And I thought—*why didn't I come up with this before?* Hills Village Elementary School had hundreds of fourth and fifth graders. What if we could turn every single one of them into a vote for We Stink?

I hated to admit it, but Rafe was right. We needed to think *big*. If we could crack the birthday party circuit, we were going to be one giant step closer to winning this whole thing.

"Hi, Mrs. Gorman," I said, like I just happened to be walking by. "I see you're having a party. How would you like some free live music? My band had a cancellation this morning, so we're available."

"Really?" she said. "Do you play music that's appropriate for children?"

"Sure!" I said. Which was true. We're not exactly a parental advisory lyrics kind of group.

"Well, that would be wonderful," she said. "I was supposed to have Shrimpy the Clown, but apparently he picked up a case of head lice at his last party, so...can you be ready in an hour?"

"Of course we can!" I said.

I thought it was a little weird for McCasalin to want a clown at her birthday, but it didn't matter now. Shrimpy's bad luck was our big break. I turned around and ran home to call the girls and get ready.

We were going to need our instruments, of course. Also Nanci's phone, for filming purposes. And something to tell people about the contest. So right after I called Mari and told her to call Patti and Nanci, I made the

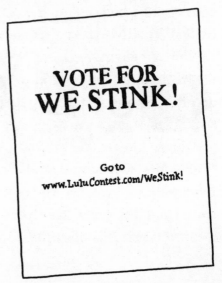

VOTE FOR WE STINK!

Go to
www.LuluContest.com/WeStink!

world's quickest flyer on Mom's computer. It wasn't great, but I didn't have time for *great*.

"What are you doing?" Rafe asked me.

"See? I can think big," I said, and handed him one of the flyers. "We're going to get every fourth and fifth grader in Hills Village to vote for us."

"Wow," Rafe said.

"Thanks," I said.

"No," he told me. "It's more like I'm starting to feel sorry for you."

"Here's an idea," I said, and snatched the flyer out of his hand. "Don't bother me about it."

It was stupid to even try and have a real conversation with Rafe. Not to mention a waste of my time. I had to get busy launching the VOTE FOR WE STINK campaign, once and for all.

"I'm just saying—"

"La-la-la-la-la-la!" I said to Rafe, as I picked up my stuff and flew back out the door. "Not listening!"

"Yeah," I heard my brother say behind me. "That's pretty much your problem, right there."

CHAPTER 16

Change of Plans

Okay, in my defense, I want to say that what happened next could have happened to anyone. It was all just a misunderstanding.

When I got back to the Gormans' house, Mrs. Gorman had her hands full. She was carrying around McCasalin's baby brother, and he was crying up a storm, so she just pointed me toward the backyard and kept moving.

Nanci was already there, setting up her drums. Patti and Mari were on the way. And the whole house smelled like cake.

As soon as I saw McCasalin, I went right over to her. She was our ticket to the rest of Hills Village Elementary, so I wanted to be especially nice and get her pumped for our show.

"Hey, McCasalin!" I said. "Happy birthday! That's a nice jacket! Did you get it as a gift?"

But McCasalin looked at me like I was speaking some kind of secret language. A bunch of other adults were just getting there, too. And the weird part was, they all had babies and toddlers with them.

"It's not *my* birthday," McCasalin said.

"Wait…what?" Mari said. She and Patti had just gotten there, too. Now everyone was staring at me.

"It's Adam's birthday," McCasalin told me, and pointed at her one-year-old brother. "I hope you guys know 'Itsy Bitsy Spider,' because that's his favorite."

"Hey, sweetie!" Mr. Gorman yelled from a car in the driveway. "The movie starts in twenty minutes. Let's roll!"

"Catch you next time!" McCasalin said, and took off, just like that.

I didn't even think about giving her a flyer until she was already gone. I was too busy noticing the way Mari, Patti, and Nanci were looking at me—like I had one big *"OOPS!"* tattooed across my forehead.

So basically, the first show of our big campaign didn't go quite as planned. I mean, we did end up with a houseful of screaming babies, but I don't think that had anything to do with the music.

Let's just say it gave our band name a whole new meaning. And not in a good way.

Mixed Messages

After that disaster, I was really looking forward to Monday after school. That's when I had my first maybe-date with Sam. And, boy, was it *romantic.* We went to the junk shop, the city dump, and the hardware store, looking for parts for our Rube Goldberg machine.

"What about this?" Sam asked, picking up a giant spring at the junk shop. "Maybe we could use it to trigger a catapult."

"And then have it toss a ball into this," I said, holding up an old butterfly net. "That could be cool."

I know, I know. Not exactly romantic. But most

of the couples I know in middle school don't even get past holding hands in the hall between classes. At least we were off school grounds.

See, I still hadn't figured out if Sam and I were friends, or more than friends, or just plain old science partners and nothing more. But it's like Mom said: "Khatchadorians don't give up easily." So while we looked for machine parts, I also tried to look for clues.

"This is all so time-consuming," I said, as casually as I could. "I wonder how real scientists find time for other stuff."

"What other stuff?" Sam asked.

"Oh, I don't know," I said. "Like having a social life. Going on dates. Or whatever."

In other words: HINT HINT HINT HINT HINT.

"Hmm," Sam said, as he picked up a rusty old hinge from one of the twenty-five-cent bins.

Just "hmm." *That was it.*

It's possible he'd gotten my drift, and maybe he was just too shy to do anything about it. But it was also entirely possible that a bin of old rusty hinges was more interesting to Sam Marks than I could ever hope to be. The point is, I had no idea.

In a perfect world, middle school boys would come equipped with a button you could press to make them tell you exactly what they were thinking at any time. But of course this isn't a perfect world.

Maybe what I really needed was a whole new kind of machine—one that would get me an A in science, a Nobel Prize, and maybe, just maybe, a boyfriend, all at the same time.

But you know what they call that, right?

Wishful thinking.

DON'T EVEN THINK ABOUT IT
JUST FRIENDS
LUKE WARM
LUKE WARMER
GETTING THERE
CRUSH-O-RAMA
HOT FOR YOU
GEORGIA, WILL YOU BE MY GIRLFRIEND???

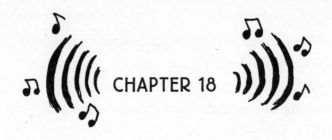

Worse Than I Thought

So if my Monday with Sam was a C-plus, then my Tuesday was more like an F. Unless there's such a thing as an F-minus.

There I was, minding my own business at school, when Missy's friend Alicia came right up to me in the hall and held out this little bag.

"I need these washed by tomorrow," she told me. "Missy said you could take care of it for me at her house this afternoon."

At first I thought Alicia must be joking. But then I remembered that the one accessory Princesses *don't* come with is a sense of humor.

"Are you seriously trying to give me your laundry?" I asked.

"Don't be ridiculous," Alicia said.

"Good," I said. "Because there's no way—"

"It's just a few delicates that need hand-washing," she said. "If I was giving you my laundry, it would be a much bigger bag."

I think Alicia actually expected me to take it. But instead, I told her where she could stick her delicates and sent her on her way.

"You haven't heard the end of this," she said.

"Whatever," I said.

About ninety seconds later, I had a face full of Missy Trillin. She came right up to me in the cafeteria.

"If I want you to wash my friends' clothes, then you're going to wash my friends' clothes," she said.

I could feel my face turning red. People were starting to stare. I wished I had a dozen fresh eggs to throw at Missy. That would give her some laundry, all right!

But lucky for me, there weren't any eggs on

hand, and I couldn't afford another punishment. So I just told her the same thing I'd told Alicia, except I gave her the spicier version. Let's just say it was somewhere north of PG-13.

And then I walked away while Missy steamed and stewed.

It felt pretty good, to be honest. But it was also only like winning a teeny-tiny battle in the middle of a ginormous war. Because I knew for a fact that Alicia's handwashables were going to be waiting for me when I got to the Trillins' that afternoon, like it or not.

In other words, I wasn't just working for one evil troll now. I was working for *all* of them.

And the only thing I could do in the meantime was make sure Missy never got to see just how badly she was driving me CRAZY.

CHAPTER 19

What's the Big Idea?

After four days online, We Stink's video was barely getting any votes at all. So far we were in forty-eighth place. Out of fifty-one entries.

And I'm not even sure the other three were real bands.

48) We Stink!
49) Asdfghjkl;
50) Ura Nidiot
51) [System Error: 404]

KEEP THOSE VOTES COMING IN!

Lulu
AND THE HANDBAGS

🐦 Tweet   f Share   ✉

I was starting to feel the pressure, big-time. Between this impossible contest and my impossible prison sentence at the Trillin estate, not to mention my homework and guitar practice, it was starting to feel a little head-explodey, if you know what I mean.

But if there's one thing I'm not, it's a quitter. (Actually, there are lots of things I'm not, like popular, or pretty, or rich. But the point is—I wasn't giving up yet.)

"The voting period is only two weeks," Mari said that afternoon at band practice. "I don't think we're going to make it."

"Come on," I said. "We still have a week and a half to get into the top twelve! We can do this!"

The truth is, nobody loves Lulu and the Handbags more than I do. Which I think meant nobody wanted this more than I did. And maybe that's why I was doing most of the work so far.

"We're going to have to pull off something drastic," Nanci said.

"Something big to get people's attention," Patti said.

"Something *really* big," Mari said.

And that's when my next idea hit me—hard. Let's call it the World's Most Unwanted Brainstorm. It was like a giant gift that came wrapped in barbed wire and poison dart frogs, with signs that said DANGER!, KEEP OUT!, and DON'T EVEN THINK ABOUT IT!

Except I *was* thinking about it. Because the truth is, my brother knows how to think big. And getting attention is one of Rafe's specialties.

So I waited until after practice. Then I went inside.

I took a deep breath.

I crossed my fingers.

I crossed my toes.

And I slowly walked toward the point of no return...the brink of disaster...the entrance to the Dangerous One's Lair...

Also known as Rafe's door.

Crossing Over to the Dark Side

So in other words," Rafe said five minutes later, "you're willing to do my homework for the rest of the year if I help you?"

"Uh...*no*," I said. "Were you even listening?"

"Oh, I was listening all right," he said. "And all I heard was the sweet sound of desperation."

I knew this was a bad idea. But now it was too late to turn around. Not until I gave it my best shot.

"Listen," I told him, "this contest comes with some prize money—"

"Prize money?" he said. Now he looked

interested, like I'd dangled a giant hot-fudge-and-dollar-bill sundae in front of him. "How much are we talking about?"

"My share would be two hundred fifty—"

"Done!" Rafe said. "You can start your internship by getting me a can of Zoom and a bag of chips from the kitchen. Or you can run to the store, if we're all out. Which we probably are."

I took another deep breath. Something told me I was going to be taking a lot of those for the next week and a half. But if I just imagined Lulu waiting for me at the end of that long, dark tunnel, I could make it through anything.

In fact, now that I had something Rafe wanted on the table, we could really get down to business.

"Slow down a second," I told him. "I have a few conditions of my own. First of all, I'm not doing anything illegal or against the rules."

"Yawn," Rafe said.

"Two. If we don't win, you don't get anything."

"No problem," he said. "I live for risk."

"Three. You have to give me a free sample first."

"Free sample? What does that mean?" he said.

"One really good idea."

"I can do that," he said.

"And, four," I told him, "the girls can't know we have a deal. They have to think that whatever you're coming up with is coming from me."

"Huh?" Rafe said.

"This is my band. My deal. My contest," I said. "And I intend to keep it that way."

And yeah, I was totally bluffing. But there was no reason to roll over and play dead from the start.

For a minute, Rafe sat there and thought about it. Actually, he was probably just thinking about what he could buy with two hundred fifty dollars, but I played along.

"Okay," he said finally. "You've already admitted that you need me, and that I'm the king of good ideas. I guess I can live with the rest."

I took one more long, deep breath. This was what you might call a choose-your-battles moment.

"What about my free sample?" I asked.

"Already got it," Rafe told me. "I'm way ahead of you."

Then he picked up his sketchbook and scribbled something really fast.

"Here you go," he said, and turned the pad around to show me. "It's just a start, but I think you're going to like it."

And I'm not going to lie. I kind of loved it.

Reality Check

I got right to work after that and did something I should have done a long time ago. I put We Stink online.

You didn't think I was leaving it *all* up to Rafe, did you? I'm not that crazy.

I started with Instagram, Snapchat, Twitter, Facebook, and Google+ accounts. Then I set up We Stink channels on YouTube and Vimeo. I made us a Wikipedia page, too, and submitted it for review. I might have exaggerated a tiny bit for that, but what can I say? Rafe had me thinking LARGE.

We Stink: The World Tour

We Stink is in the launch phase of its first-ever world tour, bringing cutting-edge music and vocals to their fans (We Stinkers) around the globe. First stop—Hills Village. Next up, who knows? Rome...Beijing... London...Honoluli...

Contents

1) ~~~~~~~~~~~~
2) ~~~~~~~~~~~~~~~~
3) ~~~~~~~~~~~~~~~~~~

Vote for We Stink here!!!

History

Shredder

The Key-master

Lo Lo

Sticks

No, really—VOTE RIGHT NOW!

After that, I went online and found a list of 122 other social media websites. That was like 122 different ways of getting more votes.

And no, I didn't sign up for all of them. Just Blogger, Reddit, Tumblr, Pinterest, LinkedIn, LiveJournal, Digg…

…Skype, Snype, Periscope, Meerkat, Pitter, Patter, Smatter, Smatter2, Pic-A-Boo…

…X-Wow, Band-O-Rama, Twoo, Zing, Wing, Bing—

"GEORGIA!"

All of a sudden, Mom was in my room.

"Huh?" I said.

When I looked up, she was standing there in her bathrobe. The clock on my laptop said 1:34 a.m., and my eyelids felt like they had tiny dumbbells pulling them closed.

"What are you doing up so late?" Mom asked.

"I guess I lost track of time."

"Is this about the Lulu contest?" she said. "Sweetie, I don't want you getting carried away."

I was going to say, "I'm not getting carried away!" But since I'd just spent the last ten minutes signing up for a Slovakian music

x

newsletter, maybe it was time to call it a night.

"The thing is, we only have ten days to get into the top twelve," I said. "I have to make sure people notice us, or I'll never meet Lulu!"

Mom came over and sat on my bed.

"Let me ask you something," she said. "If you could ask Lulu *one* question, what would it be?"

I had about eighteen thousand questions for Lulu. But if I could only ask one—

"I'd want to know what it's like to walk onstage with thousands of people screaming your name," I said.

"You wouldn't ask about the music?" Mom said. "Or the writing process?"

"You said just one question," I said.

She took my laptop and put it on the desk, and started to tuck me in like when I was little.

"I think you should worry more about what kind of musical artist you'd like to be," she said, "and maybe a little less about getting famous."

Mom's all about the art. She's a painter, and creates these really cool abstracts.

But at the same time, I'm not so sure she knows what it's like to be my age. I mean, no offense to

Mom, but she didn't even go to middle school in this century.

"We do rock and roll," I said. "Not art."

"What do you think songs are? They're poems and music," she said. "And you're so good with words. It doesn't have to be big and heavy. It just has to come from you."

"But that doesn't mean people will like it," I said.

"I'd say it's better to lose as yourself than to win as someone else," she said, and gave me a kiss good night. "Think about it."

And I would. My mom's pretty smart. But meanwhile, that didn't mean I was going to slow down on the other stuff.

Oh, no.

No, no, no, no, no.

The World Tour was still very much ON.

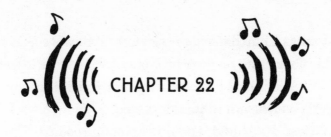
Let's Go to the Movies

When I came into the kitchen for breakfast the next morning, Rafe had his hands held up like this.

"Miss Khatchadorian!" he said. "Today is the first day of shooting on your new movie. How does it feel?"

"It feels like I just woke up and you're already being weirder than usual," I said.

"Cut!" Rafe said, and put his hands down. "I'm just practicing. Because I had an even bigger idea last night."

"Bigger than We Stink: The World Tour?" I asked.

Rafe held up his hands again. "Get this," he said. "We Stink: The World Tour: *A Rock-You-Mentary*." Then he put down his hands and looked at me. "Get it? Like a *documentary* about a *rock* band on their way to the top."

I was actually impressed. And even a tiny bit touched.

"Do you really think we can win this thing?" I asked.

"Probably not," he said. "But I'll bet Mrs. Donatello will give me credit for art class, either way."

I might have guessed.

"Flip said I could use his camera," Rafe went on. "He's got a GoBro, too. Those things are sweet! This movie's gonna be killer!"

GO BRO
THE CAMERA DUDES LOVE

"I can't afford to pay Flip, too," I said. "You'll have to share any prize money you get with him—"

"Flip's not in it for the money," Rafe said. "He has a crush on, like, half of We Stink, so basically, he's on board for anything."

"Hang on," I said. "Flip has a crush? On which half?"

"Well," Rafe said, "it's more like he *used* to think you were cute—"

"He WHAT?"

"—but I talked him out of that," Rafe said. "Now he likes Mari. And it wouldn't kill you to let her know that, by the way."

I was still stuck on the part about how Flip Savage used to think I was cute. Even if he didn't think so anymore.

I mean, it's not like I WANTED Flip to like me. The idea of going out with my brother's best friend was kind of gross. And for another thing, I liked Sam.

But still, this was good news. Because if I could be completely clueless while Flip thought I was cute, then maybe it was also possible for Sam to like me without my ever figuring it out.

That was a big maybe, but even so—

"Hello? Earth to Georgia?" Rafe waved a hand

in front of my face. "Do you want to talk about this movie idea or not?"

"Definitely," I said, snapping to attention. "So when do we start?"

"As soon as we get to school. And this afternoon, you need to get your band to City Hall Park for your first music video shoot."

Okay, I'll admit it. Rafe was on a roll.

There was only one problem.

"I can't this afternoon," I said. "I have to work at the Trillins'."

Rafe gave me this look, like I was the world's leading cause of lameness.

"What?" I said. "It's not like I'm doing volunteer work over there!"

"The day after tomorrow, then," he said. "No excuses."

Already, my brain was bubbling with ideas. But I didn't want to get *too* excited yet. This was Rafe, after all.

"I'm in," I said. "Just don't mess it up, okay?"

"What makes you think I'm going to mess anything up?" he asked.

If I could have, I would have handed him a copy of his own life story to make my point.

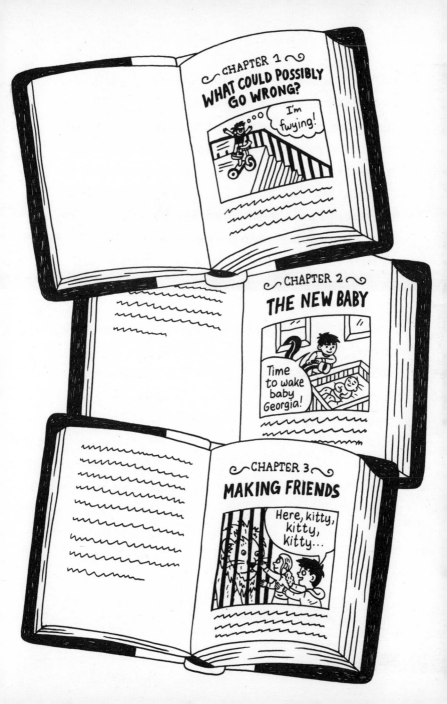

"Just remember, you work for me," I said.

"I don't think of it like that," Rafe said. "It's more like you're the engine, but I'm the gas." And just to prove it, he let one rip right there at the breakfast table.

Yeah. Because nothing inspires confidence like a game of Pass the Gas from the kid who's taking your entire future into his own hands.

Hoo, boy. What had I just gotten myself into?

CHAPTER 23

Scene One

And...ACTION!"

"I can't be-*LIEVE* that *WE* are on our *WAY* to the *TOP!*" Nanci said to me while we opened our lockers.

"CUT!"

We both stopped and looked at Rafe.

"What is it now?" Nanci asked.

We'd been working on our Rock-You-Mentary for five minutes, and Mr. Big Shot Director was already getting on our nerves.

"People are staring," I said. "Do we really have to do this in front of everyone?"

"Right," Rafe said. "Because doing this where people *won't* notice is a great way of getting famous."

I'd already gotten at least five eye rolls, although one of those might have just been Ashley Catalan's allergies acting up. Still, I felt like a fish in a fishbowl under a microscope.

But Rafe was right. If I wanted to be famous, I was going to have to suck it up and get used to it. And middle school is all about learning to be the adults we're going to be, right?

"Okay, let's do it again," I said. Right before we got slammed by a Princess hit-and-run.

"Oh, *wow!*" Missy Trillin said, oozing by in a strawberry-scented cloud. "That...is...*adorable.*"

Chloe and Alicia were there, too, of course. It's like Missy keeps them on invisible leashes.

"I wouldn't shoot more than one episode of that little reality show," Chloe said. "It's going to be canceled before it starts."

"It's not a reality show!" Mari said. "It's a documentary."

"It's a *Rock*-You-Mentary," Rafe said.

"Awwww," Missy said. "That's even more

adorable. You know—in a sad, pathetic kind of way."

"Who do you guys think you're fooling?" Alicia said. "You're just a middle school band—"

"Yeah," Chloe said. "Band of losers!"

Then someone else chimed in.

"You're the ones talking about them," Sam said. "I don't see them worrying about what *you're* up to."

I hadn't even seen him coming. He just showed up like some kind of superhero. You know, the kind with an armful of books and a ketchup stain on his hoodie.

But he was *my* superhero.

Missy and her prissy minions didn't even have a good comeback. Or anything to say for that matter.

But Mrs. Stricker sure did.

"EXCUSE ME!" she said. "Am I the only one who heard the first-period bell? Rafe, put that camera away!"

"We're making a documentary," he said. "It's for art."

"Ten, nine, eight…" she said.

"You can ask Mrs. Donatello!" Rafe said.

"Seven, six, five…"

"We're going!" I said, and we scattered before Mrs. Stricker could get anywhere near three, two, one. I didn't want to find out what came after that.

The Princesses scattered, too. I could hear them on their way to class.

"Did you study for the math test?"

"There's a math test?"

"Exactly."

"No, seriously, there's a test…?"

That was the last I heard before I stopped worrying about them and started thinking about other stuff instead. Like my science project.

And by science project, of course, I mostly mean *Sam*.

CHAPTER 24

Science Experiment

So if the tin can with the golf ball tips over here," Sam said, putting it next to an old piece of wooden train track, "the golf ball can run down the track, and knock the marble into the funnel—"

He flicked the marble into the funnel, where it spiraled around, then down through the hole—

"And onto the Return button on my laptop," I said. "Which I'll have preset to text Swifty's Diner."

Everyone in the class was using marbles and tracks and pendulums for their machines, too. But no one was making a robocall-the-diner, order-your-breakfast, and have-it-waiting-for-pickup-on-the-way-to-school…machine.

The problem was, every time that marble plopped out of the funnel, it just rolled across my keyboard and hit the floor with a dull clunk. It was like the sound of a C-minus, if you know what I mean.

"Hmm," Sam said. "Maybe we need a heavier marble."

"By the way," I told him, "thanks for standing up for us in the hall like that."

"No prob," he said, and went back to looking at the assignment sheet, while I just looked at him.

I'd been trying to figure Sam out for forever now. I talked it over with Mari, Patti, and Nanci, and they all thought that even though he hadn't asked me on a date, he liked me. And to be honest, so did I. But I needed some proof, and everything I tried just went *clunk*, like that marble on the floor.

But Mrs. Hibbs always says if your experiment isn't working, try coming at it from a different angle.

So I did.

"So, we've been working on some new songs for the band," I said.

"Cool," Sam said, and tore off a piece of duct tape.

"Yeah," I said. "The new one's called 'Do You Like Me Like That?'"

"Uh-huh," he said, taping the funnel into place.

"We also have one called 'What Are You Doing Saturday Night?'" I said. "Because I was thinking we could do something together. You know—just the two of us."

"Awesome," he said. He didn't even look up. Seriously, this boy was cute, smart, nice, and CLUELESS.

And I was running out of ideas.

#DoYouLikeMeLikeThat?

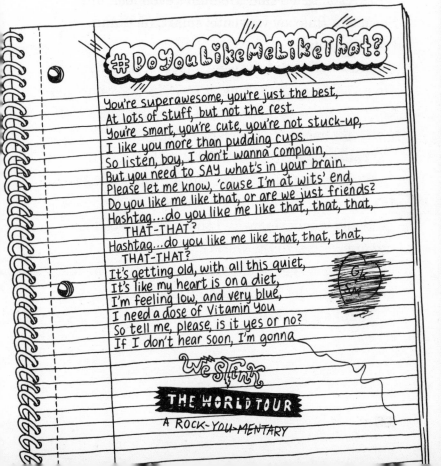

"Whatcha doin'?" Rafe asked. "Is that a new song?"

When I looked up, he was pointing his camera right at my notebook. I practically jumped eight feet, but not as fast as I slammed that notebook closed.

"NO! WHY WOULD YOU ASK THAT? IT'S PRIVATE. DID YOU SEE ANYTHING?" I said.

"Wow," Rafe said, "who put the Red Bull in your chocolate milk?"

"Nobody!" I said. "I mean...just let me know next time you point that thing at me. There's a fine line between making a movie and snooping, you know."

"Not when you're a celebrity," he said.

"I'M NOT A CELEBRITY!" I yelled.

Which was unfortunate, since I was sitting in the corner of the cafeteria. And now everyone was probably wondering why I thought I needed to announce that to the world.

If I ever do get famous, something tells me it's going to be a lot harder than it looks.

Thanks a lot, Rafe.

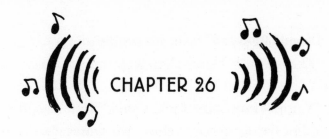

CHAPTER 26

Two to Tutor

When I got to the Trillins' that day, things with Missy got worse in a whole *new* way.

"Georgia!" Mrs. Trillin said. "Come in. I need to ask you a favor."

And I thought, what now? Oil change for the limo? Polish the burglar alarms? But that wasn't even close.

"I understand you do fairly well in school, is that right?" she asked me.

"I guess," I said. I didn't want to brag.

"Well, Melissa's math test did *not* go well," she said. "And I'm insisting that she get a tutor. So I thought as long as you're here—"

I kind of gasped. Or at least gulped.

"Excuse me?" I said. "You want me to…to…tu…."

"Tutor Missy," Mrs. Trillin said. "That's right."

And I thought—well, that's the worst idea since meatless bacon. It was bad enough working for the Princess Patrol, but tutoring would mean I had to spend every minute of my prison sentence in the same room as Missy. No, thank you!

"I don't mean to be rude, Mrs. Trillin, but you know we're not exactly friends, right?" I said.

"But, sweetheart, Missy *asked* for you," she said.

Oh. My. *Geometry*. It was even worse than I thought. This was like being invited into the alligator pit by the head alligator herself.

The question was, what torture did Missy have in mind for me now?

"I guess she knows how smart you are," Mrs. Trillin said. "Also, she needs to earn a B or better on the next quiz if she wants to get *this* back."

Then she held up a cell phone in a familiar lavender leather case.

"Ohhhh," I said. It all started adding up in my mind like…well, like a big math problem.

FACT #1: I didn't really have a choice about the tutoring. I basically had to do what Mrs. Trillin said.

FACT #2: Missy didn't really have a choice, either. Not if she wanted her phone back. (And Missy *definitely* wanted her phone back. She loved that thing more than water, air, and lip gloss combined.)

FACT #3: That meant I had something Missy needed. Also known as math skills. Which was like having Missy's fate in my hands.

"I'd be happy to help out," I said.

"Wonderful!" she said. "She's just up in her room, pouting."

(Did I mention that I was starting to like Mrs. Trillin?)

"Actually, is there a bathroom I could use first?" I asked.

I didn't really have to go. I just needed a minute to figure out what I was going to do next.

Because now, it was like I had the alligator by the jaws. That's better than the other way around, but it's also dangerous. I needed to proceed with extreme caution.

One thing was for sure, though. Opportunity had just knocked, and I intended to answer the door.

CHAPTER 27

Missy — Phone + Math x Georgia = ?????

Missy's bedroom was just as megasized as I'd expected. She had a canopy bed that was about two stories high, and a whole media center with *two* TVs. Why two? Is she afraid she'd miss out on the latest toothpaste commercial?

There was also a spiral staircase going up to a loft, with a window that looked out toward the pool house. I could live in that room and still have space for a live elephant collection.

Meanwhile, Missy was laid out on her bed like a starving castaway on a tiny, fluffy island.

I've heard that humans can last for three weeks without food, three days without water, and three minutes without oxygen. But when I got there, it looked like Missy wasn't going to make it another three seconds without that phone.

"What are you waiting for?" she said. "Let's get this over with. And you'd better be a good teacher."

"Actually," I said, "we have a little business to attend to first."

"What's *that* supposed to mean?" she said.

I stepped inside and closed the door.

"Here's the deal," I said. "I'm going to get you a B or better on that quiz. But first you're going to talk to your mom about getting me out of this whole servant deal once you pass."

Missy looked at me like I was a piece of gum stuck to her shoe.

"You can't talk to me like that," she said. "You work for me."

"Okie-dokie," I said, and turned to leave. "I'm sure you'll be just fine using your desktop and land line for the rest of the year—"

"Wait!"

I stopped with my hand on the doorknob. And that's when my house radio squawked to life.

"How's it going up there, girls?" Mrs. Trillin said. *"Do you have everything you need?"*

I picked up to answer and said, "Actually, Mrs. Trillin, I'm not sure this is going to—"

Right before Missy flew across the room on her broomstick and snatched the radio out of my hand.

"We're *greeeaaat!*" she told her mom, in her fakest, most princessy voice. "I'm getting smarter already. Aren't I, Georgia?"

"I don't know," I said. *"Are you?"*

Missy gave me a super-glare then. The kind that could wilt flowers. And probably set them on fire, too.

"Mommy, I'm coming downstairs," she said into the radio. "I need to talk to you about something first."

Then she shoved the radio back in my hand.

"Satisfied?" Missy asked.

"Actually," I said, "I could really use one of those fruit smoothies, too. Maybe pick it up on your way back?"

Missy gave me another evil look. But then she headed for the door.

"Just so we're clear," she said, "I hate you."

"Strawberry-banana would be just *greeeeaaat!*" I said. "Thanks!"

In other words, mission accomplished.

I guess maybe Rafe and I are a little bit alike, after all.

Shopping!

I was in a pretty good mood by the time I got home, even if tutoring Missy was like one of those bad dreams where you keep ending up in the same place, over and over and over....

But at least there was an end in sight. Mrs. Trillin agreed to end my prison sentence if Missy got a good grade on her quiz!

To celebrate, I scooted out to meet the girls for a little bargain shopping.

If we were going to shoot a real-live music video the next day, we wanted to look like real-live rock stars.

For about ten bucks apiece, if at all possible.

Lucky for us, Patti knew about an awesome thrift store called New2U, where we went crazy trying stuff on. So by the time we were done, we went from this...

♡ ⟲
22 likes
WeStink #beforeshot #LuluContest #VoteForWeStink!
#PleeeeeeeeaseVoteForWeStink!
#noreallydoitnow

to this...

And finally, because the lady at the counter said they were closing and we had to pick something, we ended up with this.

Not bad, right?

22 likes
WeStink #aftershot #LuluContest
#DidYouVoteForWeStinkYet #whatareyouwaitingfor
#rockinlook #only10bucks

"Do we look like rock stars?" Mari asked.

"I guess so," I said.

"But now we need to start *acting* like rock stars," Nanci said. So we trashed the store and left without paying.

Just kidding. We cleaned up after ourselves, paid, thanked the clerk, and left.

But you can bet we looked ROCKIN' AWESOME doing it.

A Lean, Clean Music Machine

The next day was the first official stop on the We Stink World Tour. I went straight from school with my guitar to meet the girls by Millennium Fountain in City Hall Park.

It was a good location. The fountain had all these splooshy jets of water that made a really good backdrop for our video. I was getting excited.

"How is this any different from the last two times we played here?" Mari asked. "We didn't get applause then. We got crickets!"

I tried to stall, since I didn't exactly know. "Well…"

"We're here! We're here!" Rafe said, just in time. He'd brought Flip, too.

"Hey, everyone," Flip said. And then, "Hi, Mari."

"Hey, Flip," Mari said, smiling, and you could just practically see their eyes turning into hearts like those emojis. Which was fine with me, because Flip was here to help. And the more people around, the better.

"What's in the backpack?" Nanci asked him.

"Oh, just some of Rafe's awesome flyers," Flip said, and pulled out a handful. They had the World Tour logo on them, along with a link for our voting page.

"Rafe's going to film, you guys are going to play, and I'm going to hand these out to people," Flip said.

"Okay, let's do this!" Rafe said.

"Do *what,* exactly?" I asked.

"You four just stand there and play. We'll take care of the rest," he said. "And no matter what happens, *don't stop.*"

That's when I started getting the creepy, tingly feeling up the back of my neck. I call it the Rafe Alarm. It's when you know something's wrong, and you know it's Rafe's fault, but you just don't know what it is yet.

"What's that supposed to mean?" I asked, right before Nanci counted us off. We'd chosen one of our rockingest songs, "Spring Cleaning," so I didn't have any choice but to start playing.

At first, a bunch of people looked over, just like the last time we played City Hall Park.

And then they all went back to ignoring us. Just like the last time. I noticed Flip had disappeared, too. Maybe even *he* was bored.

"Nothing's happening!" I told Rafe, right into the camera.

"Just give it a second," he said.

And then, sure enough…people started noticing again. Some of them came closer. Others were pointing.

It was working! Our music was hooking the crowd. Maybe Mom was right, after all, I thought. We *were* musical artists! And if I just kept focusing on my writing, then everything else would take care of itself.

Except—that's when I noticed the bubbles.

Lots and lots of soapy bubbles were filling up the fountain behind me. It looked like the world's biggest washing machine had gone berserk. And the pile was getting bigger, fast.

But so was the crowd.

"What did you do?" I asked Rafe with my back turned to everyone.

"Just go with it!" he said. Then he stuck the camera

in my face, swooped away, and got a shot of Nanci at the drums, right before the song came to an end.

"Again!" Rafe yelled. "One! Two! One-two-three-four!"

"That's my job!" Nanci said.

"Whatever! Keep playing!" he said.

The suds were spilling right out of the fountain by now. And some of the kids were climbing right in. The more they kicked around, the higher that mountain got, and the more it spilled around our feet and ankles. Pretty soon, it looked like We Stink was rocking out on top of a giant whipped-cream-covered sundae.

Three words: Awe. Some. Ness.

It was insane! In the most tremendously, awesomely bubblicious possible way.

I was still a little freaked out about how this got started, and whether we were going to get in trouble, but then the Channel 12 News van pulled up. A reporter jumped out with a cameraman behind her and they headed right for us.

It was amazing how fast they'd gotten there. I guess *someone* must have called ahead and tipped them off.

Imagine that.

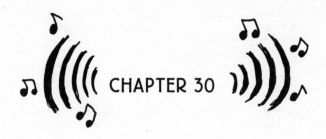

Tonight's Top Story

We had to rush home to catch the evening news, and we got there just in time.

"Turn on the TV, turn on the TV!" I said to Grandma Dotty, who was home while Mom was at work.

And then there we were.

"Good evening, I'm Carly Morehead and these are tonight's top stories. A local band's performance in City Hall Park today was interrupted by a gigantic bubble bath...."

"Hashtag omigosh!" I said. It was happening. I was on TV!

"I know that girly!" Grandma Dotty said, and hugged me really tight.

Meanwhile, Rafe was filming me while I was watching. "Sit closer to the TV," he said. "And look over here!"

"SHHH!" I said, because my interview with the reporter was just coming on.

When she interviewed me at the park, I told her all about the World Tour and the Lulu contest, and I must have said "Vote for We Stink" about twenty times.

But all they showed was a tiny little clip with my name misspelled.

This is **CRAZY!**

7 **GEORGIA KASHADOODIAN**
LOCAL MUSICIAN

That was it. But even so, it was the most famous I'd ever been. By a long shot.

As soon as the story was over, the phone rang. It was Mari calling to scream about how amazing it all was. Rafe said he was going to run over to her house and "do an on-the-spot interview."

Then the phone rang again, and it was Nanci. Everything was moving so fast!

When the doorbell rang a minute later, I thought maybe it was Patti. Or maybe another reporter. Or maybe...

Then I looked out the front window.

Some kind of official-looking car was parked outside. Not only that, but an official-looking man in an official uniform was standing at our door, waiting for someone to let him in.

And that's when I knew the fun was over.

CHAPTER 31

Not Quite Lying

In a complete panic, I ran to my bedroom to hide. I left the door open a crack so I could hear what the man said to Grandma Dotty when she opened the door.

"Hello, ma'am, I'm Officer Parks from the Hills Village PD."

Can you say "heart attack"? I felt like I was going to pass out. And, of course, Rafe was conveniently nowhere in sight—so I had no one to blame!

This was it. It finally happened. My brother had turned me into a juvenile delinquent.

"You don't look like a police officer," Grandma Dotty said, while I held on to the wall and tried not to fall over.

"Sorry," he said. "I meant the Parks Department, not the Police Department."

And I thought—*Why doesn't that make me feel any better?*

"Does Georgia Kashadoodian live here?" the man said. "I'd like to ask her a few questions."

And I thought—*Yeah, that's why.*

"I'm sorry," Grandma Dotty said. "Did you say Officer Parks? From the Parks Department?"

I heard the man take a deep breath. "Yes, ma'am. I get that a lot," he said.

Meanwhile, I was wondering how fast I could tie my sheets together and climb out the window. It wouldn't be so bad. I could live out there, on the road. Nobody would even *think* to look for me in Saskatchewan....

Or maybe not. *On the run from the law* isn't my style. (But you already knew that, didn't you?)

Still, I would have cleaned Missy Trillin's private bathroom for the rest of my life if I could have slipped out of there unseen somehow.

"Georgia, honey!" Grandma Dotty called.

So I took a deep breath. I tried to focus. And I trembled my way out to the living room.

"Hi, Georgia, I'm Officer Parks," he said.

"He's from the Parks Department," Grandma Dotty said, and I saw her trying not to laugh.

I wasn't even close to laughing. It's hard to giggle when you're trying not to panic-pee in your pants.

"Um...hi," I said. "Is this about the bubbles?"

"That's right," he said. "Do you know anything about it?"

"Well, we were making a video, and it just started...bubbling," I said.

"That much we know," he said. "But it seems like quite a coincidence, just as you were performing in the park."

"So true!" Grandma Dotty said. "It looked wonderful, don't you think?"

In case you couldn't tell, my grandma marches to the beat of her own private drummer. In a good way.

But Officer Parks wouldn't get distracted. He was staring at me as if he could pull the truth out of my brain just by using his eyes. I sure wished I knew what he was thinking.

"I was surprised when it happened," I said. Which was the truth.

But I'm not sure he believed me. All of a sudden, he looked about thirty percent meaner.

"So, you don't know who put the soap in the fountain?" he asked.

I was sweating from my armpits to my pinkie toes, and I just kept thinking—*No lying, no lying, no lying.* But I had to tell him *something.*

"The truth is…" I said. "This totally sounds like something my brother would do."

"Really?" he said, and flipped open a little pad. "What's his name?"

"Rafe Khatchadorian," I said, and even gave him the right spelling. "But the thing is, Rafe couldn't have done it. He was right there in front of us the whole time."

Officer Parks flipped his pad closed and looked annoyed.

"Excuse me, young lady, but did you see who did this or not?" he asked.

"No, sir," I said. "I didn't. I really, really didn't. I never saw anyone put any soap in any fountain."

Which was also the truth.

Officer Parks gave me one more long look that felt like it took about an hour to end. Finally, he pulled out a business card and handed it to Grandma Dotty.

"If any of you can think of anything else, let me know," he said.

Grandma Dotty took one look at his name on the card, put her hand over her mouth, and said,

"Excuse me. I think something's burning in the fridge."

Then she left the room. A second later, I heard the refrigerator open, and the slightly muffled sound of giggling.

Before I could brain-melt all the way to the ground, Officer Parks gave me one last firm look. Then he turned around and let himself out while Grandma Dotty just laughed and laughed and laughed in the kitchen.

I'm glad *someone* thought it was funny.

Well, That Explains a Thing or Two

When Rafe got home, I cornered him, dragged him into my room, and locked the door.

"Before you say a word, let me talk," Rafe said. "I knew you wouldn't go for it if I told you ahead of time. I just had to show you how awesome it could be."

"Yeah, just as awesome as a year in the state penitentiary," I said. Then I told him all about Officer Parks from the Parks Department.

Rafe thought it was funny, too.

"Am I the only one who takes things seriously around here?" I said, trying not to yell. Mom was home now, and I didn't want her getting suspicious. "I almost got *arrested!*" I whispered.

"What you *got* was a stint on the six o'clock

news," Rafe said. "Besides, we used the eco-friendly stuff. That fountain's never been cleaner."

"THAT'S NOT THE POINT!" I yelled before I could help it.

"Everything okay in there?" Mom called out.

"Fine!" I said.

When I looked back, Rafe was hooking Flip's camera up to my laptop.

"What are you doing?" I said.

"Don't you want to see the video?"

I'd totally forgotten. But now I *totally* wanted to see it.

At first, it was just us playing. We looked great in our new outfits, but otherwise there wasn't much to see. Right up until I noticed Flip lurking around the back of the fountain.

"We won't use this part, obviously," Rafe said nervously.

Uh-oh.

I saw Flip taking off his backpack. He unzipped the top, set it on the edge of the fountain, and sat down right on top of it.

That's when about a gallon of blue goopy liquid poured out.

"Wow, he must *really* like Mari," I said.

"Flip's totally crazy, in the good way," Rafe said. "He wants you guys to rock this movie more than I do, and I'm the director!"

It was like a train wreck. I couldn't tear my eyes away. I watched the whole thing straight through.

"Is this all loaded on my laptop?" I asked.

"It is now," Rafe said.

"Good," I said. Then I pressed the Erase All button on the GoBro dropdown menu and unplugged the camera.

"What are you doing?" he said. "I still have to edit that video!"

"You can do it on my computer," I said. "I'm not taking any chances."

"What makes you think it's any safer with you?" Rafe asked.

"Hmmm, let me think," I said. "There was the time you let Miller the Killer get his hands on your secret notebook."

"Well, yeah," he said, "but—"

"Then there was the time in art school when you took that kid's sculpture and it broke into a million pieces."

"That was an accident," Rafe said.

"Or the time you—"

"Okay, okay, I've got it," he said.

I probably should have just erased the whole thing from my laptop, but the rest of that video was pure gold.

Besides, I wasn't going to go to the trouble of facing down the Hills Village "PD" and nearly go to Parks Department jail, only to wind up with *nothing*. No way.

This World Tour business was turning out to be more dangerous than I thought.

Dream On

This is the part where I'm supposed to have an awesome dream, all about how famous We Stink is going to get.

It would include talk shows and stadium dates, magazine covers, endorsements for environmentally friendly laundry detergent, and, of course, an animated We Stink movie where we save the world from evil princesses, one hit song at a time.

And the dream would just go on and on like that, until I get swallowed up by fluffy pink cotton-candy clouds of joy…

Except that's not the dream I had that night. Not even close.

Instead, I dreamed that I was on a big ship, and

Rafe was holding me by my feet while I hung off the deck over the freezing ocean. If he let go, I was going to fall straight down to a watery grave.

Plus, he kept eating handfuls of buttery popcorn from a giant bucket, and his hands were getting greasier and more slippery while he tried to hold on.

There were also a few rainbow-colored llamas and talking seagulls in there. I probably ought to lay off the Skittles before bed next time.

I'm no dream expert, but it didn't take a genius to figure out what that one meant. Some part of me was scared to death about putting my fate in Rafe's hands.

So I couldn't help looking at him a little suspiciously at breakfast. Especially because he kept grinning at me like a crazy person.

"What?" I said.

"You didn't see?"

"See what?" I was still kind of mad about the dream, even if that part wasn't technically his fault.

"You should take a look at the contest website," he said. "Because *someone* just went from forty-eighth place to—"

I didn't even hear the rest. I was already running back to my room. I threw open my laptop, clicked onto the site, and—

Forty-one.

FORTY-ONE.

FORTY-ONE!

We were in forty-first place! Overnight! I've never been so excited about such a boring number in my life.

I couldn't believe it. This was actually happening. It was all like some kind of…well…
Just like a dream.
Minus the llamas.

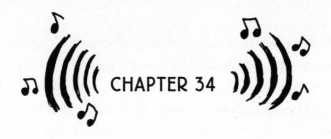

CHAPTER 34

Overnight Sensation

It kept going once I got to school, too. At least eight people said something nice to me on the way to my locker.

Usually, the only time I get noticed is when I take too long at the water fountain, or dork out at volleyball in gym and accidentally help the other team get a point.

"Georgia! I saw you on the news! Very cool."

"You're famous-ish!"

This was a whole new feeling. Like a bubbly, tiny-bit-famous, who's-that-oh-wait-that's-ME kind of feeling.

And I loved it.

"Hey, Georgia!" Jeanne Galletta said when she spotted me in the hall. "I heard you were on the news last night."

Not only is Jeanne really cool, she's also the editor of the online school paper, *Fine Print*. In other words, I was talking to another reporter now.

So I told her all about the band, and the contest, and our chance to warm up for Lulu and the Handbags.

"This is huge," Jeanne said.

"It is?"

"Sure. You guys are the biggest thing to happen at HVMS since...well, since your brother got arrested in the parking lot in the sixth grade." (Which is a whole other story, but we're talking about *me* right now.)

"Anyway, we totally have to do an interview with the band," Jeanne said.

"We do?" I said. "I mean, sure!"

She had already pulled out a little voice recorder and everything. "We're going to put you guys over the top," she said. "I'm going to make it my own personal mission."

It was still kind of sinking in. We Stink was *actually maybe* going to make it into the top twelve! That was a giant step up from definitely **not** going to make it, which is what I'd been thinking but just hadn't wanted to say out loud.

"So, Georgia, what's next for We Stink?" Jeanne asked, holding out the recorder.

And I gave her the only answer I knew.

"Everything!"

HVMS'S FINE PRINT

VOTE FOR WE STINK
CLICK HERE!

Hometown Band Bubbles to the Top!

Movie in the works!

Here's what YOU can do for We Stink!

Up next: EVERYTHING.

CHAPTER 35

Greatest Hits

Shake it, shake it!

Okay, everyone—turn up your speakers and cue the music!

This is the part where you see a bunch of quick movie scenes, one after the other, showing how We Stink really *was* bubbling to the top.

All of a sudden, we were everywhere.

37 likes
@WeStinkBand: We're in thirty-fifth place! Keep those votes coming! #LuluContest #VoteForWeStink #itsgonnahappen

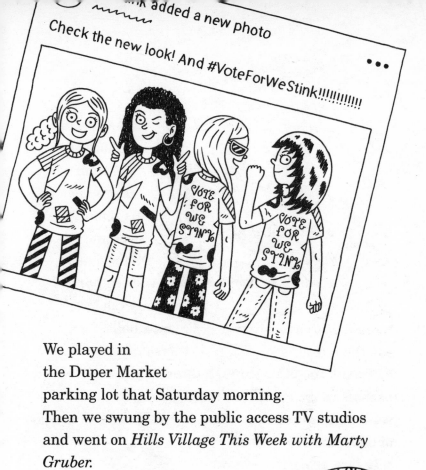

...k added a new photo

Check the new look! And #VoteForWeStink!!!!!!!!!!!!

We played in
the Duper Market
parking lot that Saturday morning.
Then we swung by the public access TV studios
and went on *Hills Village This Week with Marty
Gruber.*

We played at a pep rally at
HVMS. We also played at the
elementary school, *and* the high
school, *and* the senior center.

♪ Detention! Hate ♪ ya like lima ♪ beans! ♪♪

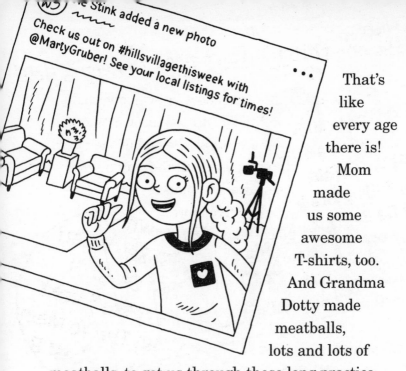

We Stink added a new photo

Check us out on #hillsvillagethisweek with @MartyGruber! See your local listings for times!

That's like every age there is! Mom made us some awesome T-shirts, too. And Grandma Dotty made meatballs, lots and lots of meatballs, to get us through those long practice sessions in the garage—I mean, in We Stink Studios. And Rafe filmed the WHOLE thing. It was all one giant team effort.

In fact, other than those tutoring sessions with Missy, it was just about the best week of my life.

We just needed a couple more

'CAUSE LIFE IS JUST A BOWL OF GREEN M&M'S!

♪ *The one thing I don't need to keep is you!* ♪

events now, or even one really big one, to put us over the top. Because by the end of the week, we'd gotten all the way up to seventeenth place.

Only five more places to go, and we were headed to Lulu-Land!

Plus...I haven't even told you one of the best parts yet.

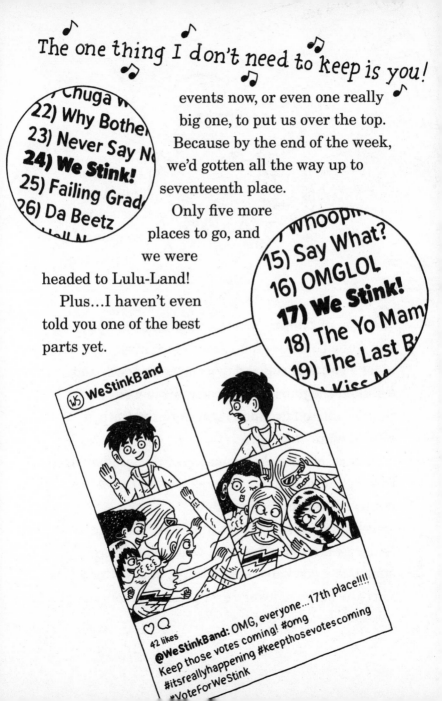

Ⓦ WeStinkBand

♡ ○ 42 likes
@WeStinkBand: OMG, everyone...17th place!!!!
Keep those votes coming! #omg
#itsreallyhappening #keepthosevotescoming
#VoteForWeStink

A...Plus

On top of everything else, Sam and I got an A on our Rube Goldberg machine that Friday!

The golf ball rolled down the train track and knocked the marble, and the marble went down the funnel and dropped right onto the Return button on my laptop.

It was like the cherry on top of the sundae. And in fact, I was about to get a cherry on top of the cherry, if you can believe that.

It happened when Sam and I were walking to lunch after science. I guess I was feeling extra sunshine-y good about everything. Maybe that's how I got the nerve to just go for it, once and for all.

"Can I ask you a question?" I said.

"Sure," he said.

"Don't think I'm weird, but…do you like me? And I don't just mean as a friend."

Sam looked at me like I wasn't making any sense.

"What are you talking about?" he said.

"Well, I said I liked *you* that day when you asked to be science partners. And then you didn't say anything back," I told him.

"Yes, I did," he said.

"Uh, no," I said. "You really didn't."

Sam looked at me again, but in a different way this time. He was turning red. Like, apple-red. Then he looked at the floor.

"I really stink at this," he said. "Now I feel stupid."

Which made me feel bad.

"It's okay if you don't like me, too," I said.

"No," he said, "it's not that. It's more like…well…I kind of thought you were already my girlfriend."

Believe me, that was *not* what I expected him to say. I would have been less surprised if he'd said, "I'm the reincarnation of your goldfish Squashy who you ate when you were three. Thanks for nothing."

"Wait. *What?*" I said.

"I'm so embarrassed," he said, even though now I was the one turning red.

"So, are you...are we...boyfriend and girlfriend?" I asked, still not sure about, well, *anything*.

Sam shrugged. "Do you not want to be?"

"No!" I said. "I mean—YES! I do. Want to. Be... you know."

And then some even crazier part of me took over. I can't even explain it, but I leaned in, and I kissed Sam right there on the stairs.

If I had thought about it, I probably would have remembered that we were...oh, I don't know...AT SCHOOL. Also that Mrs. Stricker has a habit of showing up out of nowhere.

Like, for instance, at that very moment.

You would have thought we were running around naked from the way she started yelling about it, too.

"EXCUSE ME! WHAT IS GOING ON HERE?"
she hollered.

Which is basically like Mrs. Stricker's favorite
song, if she had one.

"No public displays of affection are allowed in
school!" she said. "Let's go, you two—march!"

And just like that, I was in trouble again. Except this time, I didn't even care. Not one little bit. And I don't think Sam did, either.

CHAPTER 37

SAMSAMSAM

I barely had any time to freak out about how crazy it was that I, Georgia Khatchadorian, had a boyfriend. *My boyfriend.* That was always something other people could say, not me.

Except now—YES, ME. It was SO STRANGE. I had NO WORDS.

Actually, that's not true. I had a lot of words going through my head, but most of them were "Sam," "Sam," and "Sam."

Did I know what to do next, or how the whole girlfriend-boyfriend thing was supposed to work? Well, no. Not exactly. But then again, neither did Sam. Also known as MY BOYFRIEND.

SAM.

SAM.

SAM!

(Sigh. I was *really* happy. Can you tell?)

But like I said, I didn't get to enjoy all that for very long before a major case of trouble reared its head again.

Or maybe I should say *her* head.

You notice how short this chapter is? Well that's about how long it took for Missy Trillin to make her next move. And this one was going to be a doozy.

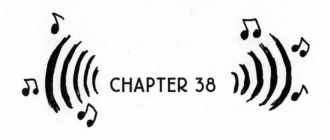

CHAPTER 38

Turning Tables

It happened in the middle of our next tutoring session, just after I tried to show Missy how to calculate the area of a right triangle.

"So," I said, "you need to divide *ab* by…?"

"Eighty-four?" Missy said.

I tried not to smack my forehead.

"Two," I said.

"Whatever," she said.

I knew Missy was smarter than this. I mean, she knew all seventy-five flavors of Lip Bomb Lip Balm by heart. And we only had to know eight formulas for the quiz.

She just wasn't trying. And I wasn't sure why.

"I need a bathroom break," I said.

"Not in *my* bathroom," she said, and pointed at the door. Which was fine with me. Really, I just needed a Missy break.

So I hiked all the way down to the powder room on the first floor and took my time.

When I got back, Missy was pointing and laughing at something on her desktop computer. Then she looked at me and laughed even harder.

I looked over at the window seat, and my laptop wasn't where I'd left it. It was sitting open on the floor. And that's when I started getting scared.

"What is that?" I asked.

"I think you know," she said.

I looked closer. Right there on her screen, plain as day, I could see Flip pouring laundry detergent into Millennium Fountain all over again.

I immediately panicked.

She had evidence! She had the proof! "That's stealing!" I said, picking up my laptop.

"And *that's* vandalism," Missy said, pointing at the screen again.

"How'd you—" I said, but I was pretty sure I knew.

"Every time you go to the bathroom, I check your laptop. And guess what? I just found a gold mine," Missy said. "Ha! Ha! Ha-ha-ha-ha-ha!"

"You're not even laughing. You're just saying 'ha.'"

"Like that's the point," she said. "Now listen to me very carefully. You're going to sit next to me in that math quiz. And you're going to make sure I can see every last one of your answers. Otherwise, this little home movie of yours is going straight to the police."

"I can't do that!" I said. "That's cheating!"

"Oh, right, because you're so above cheating," she said, and pointed at the screen again. "I don't think so."

Missy was like a supervillain. No, not even. She was like the person who trains all the supervillains and makes them cry and beg for mercy before she builds them back up again. Like a criminal mastermind. She was that evil.

Or that good, depending on how you looked at it.

I knew I couldn't do this. I couldn't knowingly let Missy cheat off me, because that would make me as bad as her. But I also couldn't imagine throwing away everything we'd worked so hard for. And the test was only three days away.

That gave me seventy-two hours to do something about this.

But *what?*

CHAPTER 39

Band Aid

I couldn't concentrate at band practice. My head was everywhere *but* in the studio, and it felt like I was trying to play my guitar with two big mittens on my hands.

I had Missy on the brain.

"Let's try that again," Nanci said. "And Georgia, pay attention. We need to get this right."

"Oh, and by the way," Mari said, "we still need to come up with a couple more events to get votes. We're so close, you guys! We can't blow it now."

"Actually," I said, "I need to tell you all something."

I couldn't stand it anymore. This was going to

explode in my face, and they'd never forgive me if it did.

So I put my guitar down and took a deep breath.

Then I told them all about what had happened. We'd never talked about who put the bubbles in the fountain, so I started at the beginning, and explained how it was Rafe's idea and how Flip had been the one with the soap.

Then I told them about Missy—every last detail.

"I'm really sorry," I said. "I was trying to keep you all out of it, but I guess I can't."

"Um...*duh?*" Patti said. "Of course Flip did it."

"You all knew?" I asked.

They all nodded.

"Well, I'm still really sorry," I said.

"It's not your fault," Nanci said.

"It kind of is," I said. "I should have just erased the video. And I should have been more careful with Missy."

"It's impossible to be careful with witches," Patti said.

"And you know what else?" Mari said. "You need to stop trying to do everything. No offense, Georgia, but you're not in charge. We're in this together."

"I know," I said. I was blushing, and my eyes were getting kind of stingy and wet. These girls were the best.

"Thanks, you guys," I said. "But what can I...I mean, what can *we* do about this?"

"Well, Rafe was the big idea guy in the park," Patti said. "What would he do now?"

"I don't want to get Rafe involved," I said. "That's like bringing a lit match to the dynamite party. He'd just mess it all up, all over—"

But then...oh. My. Brainstorm. A giant lightbulb went on in my head.

Thanks to Patti's question (and Rafe's trouble-making), I was getting an idea.

I didn't *have* to get Rafe involved. I just had to *think* like him. Which, to be honest, was starting to feel more and more like thinking like *me*.

"Georgia?" Nanci said, and waved a drumstick in front of my face. "Are you still there?"

"I've got it!" I said. "I mean, I don't want you to think I'm taking charge or anything, but I know what we have to do now. And I need all of your help to get it done."

CHAPTER 40

Infiltration Station

Buzzzzzzz!

I stepped back from the buzzer at the Trillins' gate, shushed the girls, and waited for someone to answer.

"Alloo?" a voice said. It was Nicole, the Trillins' French cook. I knew Mrs. Trillin had aquarobic yoga at her gym on Tuesday afternoons, so the timing was perfect.

"Hi, it's Georgia Khatchadorian," I said.

"Oui-oui," she said, "Come *een,* Georgia! You are here for the tutoring?"

"I'm here, all right," I said.

And the gate swung open.

Then the girls and I swung into action. We headed up the driveway but cut around the big oak tree, under the arbor on the side of the house, around the long way, and back toward the pool, where we had a perfect view of Missy's bedroom window up above.

I waved at the gardener. He was used to seeing me around, too. But still, we had to work fast. So the second we were all set up with our instruments, Nanci counted us off.

"One, two, one-two-three-four!"

We started with "Green M&M's." It didn't really matter which song we started with, as long as it was loud.

Pretty soon, Nicole came out from the kitchen.

"What *ees zis?*" she yelled.

"It's okay!" I shouted back to her. "Missy asked for it!"

Which technically, again, was true. She did ask for it!

We didn't even get to the second verse before Missy's window slammed open up above.

"WHAT DO YOU THINK YOU'RE DOING?" she screamed at us.

"CAN'T HEAR YOU!" Patti yelled.

"I SAID...*WHAT*...ARE...YOU...*DOING?*" We just ignored her and kept right on playing.

And setting the trap.

CHAPTER 41

Turning Tables, Part 2

If there's one thing Missy Trillin hates, it's being ignored. I knew she'd want to come down and personally kick us out. I was counting on it, anyway.

I also knew the house well enough to know that she'd use the back stairs and come out through the family room.

So as soon as she closed her window, I left the girls to keep playing and went in through the kitchen.

Nicole looked completely confused by now.

"Is Missy upstairs?" I asked, even though I knew the answer.

"I believe zo," Nicole said, and I kept moving. I went down the first-floor hall, up the main stairs,

back down the second-floor hall, and then *very carefully* into Missy's deserted room.

I could already hear her outside, yelling at the girls. It wasn't going to be long before she figured out what was up. I had to work ultrafast.

So I threw myself at Missy's computer. Luckily, I knew exactly what to look for. And I'd watched her log on enough to figure out her password, too.

Still, the clock was ticking. Missy had already stopped shouting, which meant she was on her way back. I could practically hear that *Mission: Impossible* theme song in my head.

My fingers flew over the keyboard. I opened
a search window and looked for anything with
"STINK" in it.

That did the trick. There was the video, right
there. I didn't even have to open it.

Right click!

Move to Trash!

And—SLAM!

"WHAT ARE YOU DOING IN HERE???!!!"

I turned around and Missy was standing there,
sweating all over the fluffy white carpet, with a
Kill-Georgia look in her eyes.

"What do you think I'm doing?" I said. "It's
already done."

Except then I realized—it wasn't. I still had to
empty the trash on her computer, or she could just
get the video back again.

I turned back to the mouse while Missy charged.

Right click!

Empty Trash!

She got there a microsecond too late. That file
was gone, gone, gone—and just in time.

"I'm calling the police!" she said. "You just stole
my property!"

"Wrong," I said. "I erased the property YOU stole from me!"

"So what?" she said. "You can't prove it."

"You also tried to blackmail me into helping you cheat," I said.

"Yeah, and I'm warning you right now," she said. "You'd better give the answers on that quiz if you know what's good for you. I can make your life very difficult if I want to."

"Actually," I said, "I don't think you will."

"Watch me," she threatened.

"Oh, I am," I told her. "And so is that little camera right there."

I pointed at the GoBro I'd left running on the desk. The one that was pointed her way and capturing the whole conversation.

"Those cameras are tiny, but they get great sound quality," I said.

"Give me that!" she said, and dove for it.

But I was one step ahead. I may limp a little when I walk, but I knew exactly what I was doing. I jumped up from the desk, grabbed the camera, ran to the window, and threw it open.

"Nanci!" I said. "Right here!"

Then I tossed the camera down to her. Nanci plays Little League *and* drums. She's got good hands. That's why we made her the catcher.

And she snagged my toss, no problem.

Missy was practically hyperventilating by now.

"Don't worry," I said. "Your secret's safe with me. I'll even help you finish studying for that quiz, if you want. But there *is* going to be one more tiny thing."

Missy looked like she wanted to explode. But we weren't quite done yet, and she knew it.

"What do you want now?" she asked.

CHAPTER 42

You're Invited

WE STINK

Is Throwing A Party—AND YOU'RE INVITED!

Come one, come all, to a fabulous pool party, concert, and video launch for WE STINK, at the even-more-fabulous Trillin Estate! Free Food, Music, Games, Prizes! And, of course, a Voting Booth where you can help put us over the top and send us to the live auditions. **AND DID WE MENTION THE FREE FOOD???** Bring your suits, your appetites, and your internet-enabled devices. We Stink will play all our greatest hits by the pool. It's gonna be

a-maaaaa-zing!

Parrr-tay!

That Saturday, we had our Pizza-Pool-Party-Palooza for We Stink at Missy's mansion. Everyone at school knew that invitations to the Trillin estate were about as common as Willy Wonka's Golden Tickets, so we had a HUGE crowd.

Even Missy was in a good mood...for Missy. She'd gotten a B-plus on her math test, thanks to our extra tutoring sessions, and that meant she was finally reunited with her boyfriend—I mean, her phone.

Her reunion with it was kind of like watching a cheesy romance movie, except that it was with, you know, a *phone*.

It's not like Missy and I were friends now. Or
even frenemies. But at least we had a truce, and
that's all I needed. Because the party was capital-
A-plus AWESOME.

Sam, Flip, and Jeanne all helped out. Each one
of them set up a voting table for us in a different

spot—by the Trillins' front gate, by the food table, and in front of the pool house.

So in other words, if you wanted to get into the party, you had to vote. If you wanted to eat, you had to vote. If you wanted to swim, you had to vote. That part was Sam's idea, and it was genius.

Meanwhile, We Stink played all our greatest hits by the pool. It was like a college party on spring break, but without any of the R-rated behavior. Unless the *R* stands for Rafe.

After our first set, I heard him shouting from somewhere over my head.

"Hey, everyone, up here!"

I looked up and he was on the roof of the pool house, pointing his camera down at the crowd.

"Everyone say 'We Stink!'" Rafe yelled.

"We Stink!" a bunch of people yelled.

Rafe yelled back. "I can't hear you!"

"WE STINK!" everyone yelled.

"One more time!"

"WE STINK!"

Part of me wanted to yell at him to come down and stop embarrassing me. But on the other hand, I know an amazing movie moment when I see one.

The music was jamming. Everyone was having a great time. Rafe was catching it all on camera. And the votes were pouring in.

In other words, We Stink was officially ready for takeoff!

Down to the Wire

By the end of the party, we'd gotten all the way to fourteenth place. Only two more spots to go before we made it into the live finals! But the voting was closing at midnight that night.

This was going to be a squeaker.

As soon as I got home, I went to my room, closed the door, and started checking the contest results every couple of minutes. Or more like every couple of seconds.

I also opened up a group chat with Mari, Patti, and Nanci.

PATTI: What place are we in now?

MARI: Can't you see?

PATTI: I'm too nervous to look! My eyes are shut!

NANCI: Huh?? But then how can you…never mind.

GEORGIA: Still in fourteenth place.

For a long time, nothing changed. We just stayed right there in fourteenth place while I refreshed and refreshed and refreshed that page until my thumb was ready to fall off.

But just after eleven thirty, something amazing happened. We jumped two spots, right into twelfth place.

MARI: Did you see that???

PATTI: See what?

GEORGIA: 12!!!!!!!!!!

PATTI: IS THIS A DREAM???

NANCI: It can't be. None of us are asleep!!

MARI: I'm delirious.

NANCI: Hi, delirious, I'm Nanci.

PATTI: How much time left??

GEORGIA: Twenty-three minu—

I didn't even get to finish typing before we moved again—down to thirteenth place.

MARI: NOOOO!

PATTI: Now it's a NIGHTMARE.

But then we popped back up to twelfth.

NANCI: YESSSSSSSSSS!!!!!!

PATTI: I can't take much more of this!

MARI: How much longer now?

GEORGIA: Twenty-two and a half minutes.

Those next twenty-two and a half minutes
felt more like years. I think I grew my first gray
hairs, just watching We Stink flip from twelfth, to
thirteenth, to twelfth, to thirteenth.

And then, with only ninety seconds to go, we
double-jumped—into eleventh place.

GEORGIA: YOU GUYS!!!!

NANCI: I'm gonna pass out!

MARI: I'm gonna pee my PJs.

PATTI: I'm gonna do both!

MARI: Almost there!!!

NANCI: But not yet!

MARI: BUT ALMOST!!!!!!!

Finally, it came down to the last seconds: ten, nine, eight, seven, six, five, four, three, two, one...

The clock on my computer clicked over to midnight....

I hit Refresh one last time....

And that's when I screamed.

MARI: ELEVENTH?

NANCI: ELEVENTH!!!!

PATTI: ELEVENTH!?!?!?!?!?!?!?!?

GEORGIA: ELEVENTH!!!!!!!

MARI: :-))))))))))))))))

The door to my room flew open, and Mom, Grandma, and Rafe all piled in. Grandma Dotty had a meat tenderizer held up like a weapon and Rafe had his camera. (So I guess I know who is going to save me from the murderers when they come and who is just going to put it in a movie.)

"What's wrong?" Mom said.

"NOTHING!" I screamed.

"But…"

"Eleventh place?!" Rafe said, looking at my laptop. Even he was excited. We might have even hugged or something.

Yeah, right.

"We're going to the live finals! And I'm going to meet Lulu and the Handbags!" I yelled, hopping up and down.

"I love a good handbag!" Grandma Dotty said.

Nobody was even mad about me waking them up. In fact, we broke out the leftover party food and had a pizza toast right there, in the middle of the night.

I hoped the downstairs neighbors didn't mind. Because none of us was going back to sleep anytime soon.

CHAPTER 45

Four Steps Forward, One Step Back

The next bunch of days went by in a blur of almost-famousness. We practiced whenever we could, shopped for new (used) clothes, and even did lots of interviews. By which I mean that Jeanne Galletta interviewed us three times.

Anything we could do to spread the word would only help us later. And Rafe said it all made pretty good B-roll for our Rock-You-Mentary. I guess he's right about some things.

Rarely.

I also wrote like crazy, trying out every new song idea I could think of.

NUT-FREE TABLE

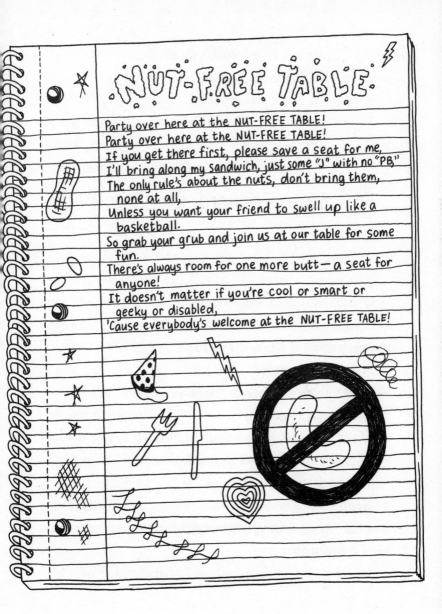

Party over here at the NUT-FREE TABLE!
Party over here at the NUT-FREE TABLE!
If you get there first, please save a seat for me,
I'll bring along my sandwich, just some "J" with no "PB"
The only rule's about the nuts, don't bring them,
  none at all,
Unless you want your friend to swell up like a
  basketball.
So grab your grub and join us at our table for some
  fun.
There's always room for one more butt— a seat for
  anyone!
It doesn't matter if you're cool or smart or
  geeky or disabled,
'Cause everybody's welcome at the NUT-FREE TABLE!

By Thursday, I was ready to explode. I couldn't wait for the finals on Saturday....

And then Friday happened.

When I got to school that morning, I noticed a familiar official-looking car parked out front. And when I walked past the office, I saw a familiar face in the hall.

It was Officer Parks from the Parks Department.

Oh. My.

Unexpected twist.

I thought he was done with his "suds mountain" investigation. But maybe not.

"Good morning, Miss...Kashadooshian," he said, looking at that little detective's pad of his.

"Khatchadorian," I told him.

"That's what I meant," he said, and scribbled something down.

"Are you here about the...bubbles?" I asked him. "I thought that was all finished."

"Just because you haven't seen me doesn't mean I haven't kept busy," he said. Then he smiled at me, the same way a cobra might smile at an extra-chubby mouse.

So I got out of there while I still could. But

something told me we weren't done with the nasty surprises that morning.

And we weren't. In the middle of first period, Mrs. Stricker got on the PA system.

"Excuse the interruption," she said. "Flip Savage, please report to the office."

It's not like she said, "Flip Savage, please report to the office for interrogation and arrest." But she didn't have to. As soon as I heard Flip's name, I knew exactly what was going on.

FACT: Flip was the one who poured that soap into the fountain at City Hall Park.

FACT: The only people who knew about it were Flip, Rafe, We Stink, and one other person. One extra-mean, strawberry-scented, fashion-plated T. rex of a human being, with the initials M.T.

FACT: My truce with Missy Trillin had just expired like a month-old bottle of milk.

FACT: I had to do something about this. *Right now.*

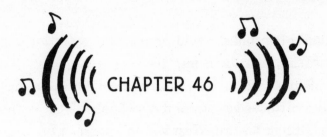

Damage Control

I couldn't let Flip just hang in the wind. He only put that soap in the fountain for the sake of *our* video. The right thing to do was march down to the office and turn myself in, ASAP.

But not before I dealt with Missy.

"Mr. Burdick?" I asked, raising my hand. "Can I go to the bathroom?"

"You can wait," he said. "The period's almost over."

Normally, I would have been a good girl and left it at that. Except I didn't have time for *good*. I needed to be just a little bit bad.

"Mr. Burdick?" I said.

"What now, Georgia?" he asked.

"I don't feel so well," I said. I put my hand over my mouth and puffed out my cheeks. "I think the eggs I had for breakfast weren't so fresh."

"Do you need a bucket?!" he asked, looking around. Cara Snow grabbed the trash can.

"I think I can…get to the bathroom," I said, and made a few little pukey sounds for good measure.

"Just go!" Mr. Burdick said. So I went.

I didn't go to the bathroom, though. I went straight to my locker, pulled out my laptop, and sat down right there in the hall.

Missy wasn't the only one with a dangerous secret. I still had that recording from when she tried to blackmail me into cheating. I also had her mom's e-mail address from my prison sentence days. So I fired off a quick message.

Dear Mrs. Trillin,

I hate to be the cause of any trouble, but my conscience won't let this rest. I am attaching the recording of a conversation I had with Missy before last week's math quiz. I think it speaks for itself.

Sincerely,

Georgia Khatchadorian

P.S. Thank you again SO much for the pool party!

As soon as I clicked Send I was on the move again. I knew Missy had computer lab first period, and I wanted to tell her about this, face to lying two-face.

"Excuse me, Mrs. Longine?" I asked when I got to the lab. "I'm supposed to bring Missy Trillin to the office."

Missy looked at me like I was a bad smell that had just floated into the room. She knew I was lying, but I could tell she was curious.

"What's this about?" Mrs. Longine asked.

"I don't know. Mrs. Stricker just said we should come right away," I told her, and then waited in the hall.

As soon as Missy came out, I pounced.

"I thought we had a deal," I said.

"Are you obsessed with me or something?" Missy said. "I don't know what you're talking about."

"You know as well as I do why Flip Savage got called to the office," I told her.

Missy scoffed and flipped her hair in my face. "I don't care *who* gets called to the office, as long as it's not me," she said.

"Don't bother playing dumb," I said. "I just wanted to let you know that your mom's going to be getting a certain message from me anytime now."

"Excuse me?" she said.

At that exact moment, Missy's precious phone dinged. She looked down at it, and there was a new text waiting for her. Probably from her mom.

"WHAT DID YOU DO?" Missy said.

"Let's just say you probably won't be burning through your data plan anytime soon," I told her.

Then I took off for the office. It would have been fun to stick around and watch Missy self-destruct, but I didn't have the time. I still had to save Flip.

Or, as my brother might say—this mission wasn't over yet.

CHAPTER 47

And the Surprises Just Keep on Coming. Not in a Good Way.

I was almost to the office door when someone grabbed me, pulled me back, and dragged me around the corner.

It was Rafe.

"Where have you been?" he said.

"Let go!" I said. "I have to get to—"

"The office, yeah, I know," he said. "But I came here to stop you."

"What is this, a Terminator movie?" I said. "Flip needs our help!"

"Just listen!" Rafe said. He checked over his

shoulder and then went on in a whisper. "Flip is the one who tipped off that Parks Department guy."

"What?" I said "Why?"

"We got it all figured out," Rafe said. "Officer Parks came to the house again last week asking even more questions. I didn't tell you because I knew you'd flip out. Flip's going to take one for the team. And you four are going to chip in ten bucks an hour for whatever they make him do."

This was all moving too fast, even for me.

"But...he could get in big trouble," I said.

"Nah. They'll just make him pick up trash in the park for a couple of hours," Rafe said. "It'll be like five bucks each."

If this were about anything besides punishments, I would have thought my brother didn't know what he was talking about. But he's pretty much an expert in that department.

And besides, Flip wasn't the problem anymore. Not even close. Because I'd just picked a major fight with Missy for no good reason.

In other words, I'd just reactivated the meanest girl in Hills Village, along with her army of spies and unlimited resources. Missy wasn't going to stop now until the Princess Patrol hunted me down, dead or alive.

I wasn't even sure which sounded worse.

Lying Low in High Places

I didn't tell Rafe a thing. It was too risky.

I couldn't tell the girls, either. Not on the day before the Lulu finals. And not after everything I'd already put them through.

The only person I *could* talk to was Sam. So I dropped a note in his locker and told him where to find me. Then I did something that I've never done before.

I skipped class.

If I wanted to avoid seeing Missy, then I had to avoid being seen, period. Her spies were everywhere.

I ducked out the nearest side door and hid behind the gym until Sam came to find me. While I waited, I tried to think of a way to undo my own stupidity.

Dear Missy,

My bad! How do you feel about ~~docovers?~~ No

Dear Missy,

~~Look on the bright side. I've heard that cell phones can be bad for your brain.~~ No

Dear Mrs. Trillin,

~~WARNING! A viral worm has infected my computer. To avoid electrocution or possible injury, please delete all incoming email without reading it!~~ NO

Dear Mrs. Trillin,

~~You may find this hard to believe, but someone has been impersonating me online.~~ NO

Dear Brazilian Embassy,

~~I am writing to ask about citizenship in your country, effective immediately.~~ NO

Dear Lulu and the Handbags,

~~Please find enclosed my application for adoption.~~ NO

"What are you doing out here?" Sam asked, and I jumped. I didn't even hear him coming.

"Avoiding a natural disaster," I said. "Also known as Hurricane Missy."

Sam didn't make me feel bad when I told him the whole story. He just listened carefully, thought about it, and came up with a sensible solution. Just like in science class.

"Well, you can't stay here," he said. "Someone's going to find you. Come on."

"Where are we going?" I asked.

"I know a place," he said, and we took off toward the playing fields.

A minute later, we were under the bleachers by the track. And then Sam started climbing, with me right behind.

At the top, there was an announcer booth where people ran the scoreboard and called the games. But it was locked the rest of the time.

"In here," Sam said.

He pushed one of the floorboards out of the way, and we climbed right up inside.

"How did you know about this?" I asked. "I thought you didn't play sports."

"I don't," he said. "I'm the track and field statistician."

"Oh," I said. That made more sense.

"Also, you're not the only one who ever had to get away from bullies," he said.

I felt like little hearts were shooting right out of my eyes and bouncing off of Sam's cute face. This wasn't exactly a romantic moment, but he *was* killing it in the boyfriend department.

"So, what do I do about Missy?" I asked.

"Nothing for now," Sam said. "You need to focus on We Stink until the live finals are over."

We decided I'd stay out of sight until the end of the school day. Saturday was the finals, and we were leaving for the city at the crack of dawn. Then on Sunday I'd explain everything to Mom and beg for forgiveness. I'd probably still get in some trouble, but right now I had to prioritize.

1. The live finals
2. Everything else

So that was the plan. I'd worry about Missy after the weekend. I mean, unless We Stink won the whole competition, got instantly famous, went out on tour, and never had to come back to Hills Village ever again.

Because, hey, you never know.

CHAPTER 49

Road Tripping

It wasn't easy, but I made it all the way to the next morning without a full-scale Missy Trillin attack.

At 6:00 a.m., we piled into two vans and took off for the big city. Mom, Rafe, and Grandma Dotty took the equipment in our car, and I went with the girls and Nanci's dad in their van.

Still, I didn't breathe a sigh of relief until I saw the THANKS FOR VISITING HILLS VILLAGE sign on the edge of town. In fact, I don't think I breathed at all.

"You're awfully quiet," Patti said. "What's wrong?"

"I'm just nervous," I said.

"Who isn't?" Mari said. "Maybe we should practice."

The song we'd picked for the finals was "Let's Shake on It," but with a new arrangement. This was the biggest thing any of us had ever done, so we decided it was only fair to split up the lead vocals.

"What's my first line again?" Patti asked.

"'I'm your girl, watch me twirl,'" I told her.

"No, that's *your* line," Mari said. "Patti's line is 'You're my guy, I'll watch you fly.'"

"Oh gosh, what if we forget?" Patti said.

"Maybe we should have practiced more," I said.

"You guys! We'll be fine!" Nanci said. "Just remember to come in together on the chorus."

We'd worked out some cool harmony for that part, too, and tried it again in the car.

"Let's shake on it!" we sang. "Shake-a-shake-a-shake-a-shake, let's shake on it!"

"Okay, *that* sounded amazing," Nanci said. Which it actually did.

But still, I kept thinking about Missy popping out of a guitar case to strangle me. Or showing up backstage with a couple of hired hit men. Or using her Trillin money to shut down the city completely.

Between all that, and the fact this was THE BIGGEST DAY OF MY LIFE, I was shaking, all right.

Straight out of my two-dollar thrift-store super-cool rock-and-roll boots.

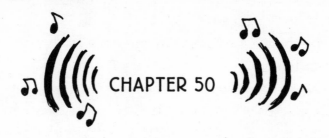

CHAPTER 50

Welcome to the Big Time

From the second we got out of the car in front of the theater, they kept us moving.

There were people in red Lulu sweatshirts everywhere, herding kids and instruments from the street into the lobby. It wasn't exactly the red carpet, but it was incredibly exciting.

Inside, the theater itself was GI-GAN-TIC. It felt like walking into the Grand Canyon. In a cool, exciting, and completely terrifying kind of way.

Meanwhile, everywhere I looked, there was another band of kids who seemed cooler or more confident or more talented or better dressed than us.

Or all of the above. I just hoped we didn't get eaten alive by the competition.

"Georgia, how are you feeling?" Rafe asked, sticking his camera in my face.

I wanted to say, "I feel like throwing up." But this was for our Rock-You-Mentary, so I just said, "I feel awesome! Let's do this!"

Pretty soon, a voice boomed over a microphone out of nowhere.

"EXCUSE ME, EVERYONE! PLEASE TAKE YOUR SEATS. BAND MEMBERS IN THE FIRST FIFTEEN ROWS, FAMILY IN THE LAST FIFTEEN ROWS, BEHIND THE YELLOW TAPE. WE WILL BE STARTING SHORTLY, SHORTLY, VERY SHORTLY!"

It was all a blur now. Mom and Grandma Dotty hugged me and wished us luck.

"You're going to do great, honey!" Mom said. "Don't be nervous."

But I was trembling like a plate of Jell-O in an earthquake. "Everyone else looks so...*ready,*" I said.

"I'll tell you a secret," Mom said. "A lot of these kids are thinking the same thing—that *everybody else* looks like they know exactly what they're doing."

"I doubt that," I said.

"Just focus on being yourselves," Mom said. "It got you this far, right?"

"Come on, Georgia, we've got to go!" Patti said.

And I decided right there that Mom was right. We'd made it into the top twelve, after all. This was our chance to do something amazing, whether or not we won the whole thing.

And who knew? Maybe...just maybe...we'd surprise them all.

Starting with ourselves.

CHAPTER 51

Here Comes the Judge

As soon as everyone was in their seats, the lights in the theater went down. A spotlight hit the stage, and some guy I'd never seen before walked into the light.

"Goooooooood morning, Lulu fans!" he shouted into his microphone.

He was wearing a shimmery gold jacket and had a purple stripe up the middle of his hair.

"I am your head judge, Jordy Swivel," he said.

A bunch of people applauded, mostly from the parents' section.

"Thank you, thank you!" he said. "Some of you

may know me from my number one hit single, 'Angel in Neon Legwarmers.'"

"From which century?" Patti whispered.

Nanci was already looking him up on her phone and showed me a picture.

Jordy Swivel 1982

"In just a few minutes, we will move you backstage, where you'll wait to be called for your individual performances," Mr. Swivel told us. "Meanwhile, remember, you are here to make great music."

I squeezed Mari's hand. My stomach was still doing Olympic gymnastics, but at least my breakfast was staying put.

"We want to hear what YOU can do," Mr. Swivel said. "Not what someone else can do."

And I thought—wow, he sounds just like Mom.

"This is a serious competition," he went on. "And it comes with a serious prize."

That was true, too. No matter what else happened, we were going to meet Lulu and the Handbags tonight!

"So if you're not scared to death right now, you're doing something wrong," Mr. Swivel said. "Because, trust me, kids, rock and roll is a vicious business. There's always someone ready to throw you under the bus, max out your credit card, and skip town with your girlfriend in Milwaukee when you least expect it—"

A woman ran onto the stage. She had a headset and a clipboard, and she whispered something to Mr. Swivel.

"Right! Yes!" he said sheepishly. "So as I was saying, the most important thing today is to have fun! Am I right?"

We all sort of applauded. Sort of nervously.

"Then let's get this party started!" he said. "Good luck everyone, and I'll see *you* ON STAGE!"

Special Delivery

Here's another fact for you. The room where you wait backstage is called the green room, but there's nothing green about it. It was just folding chairs, bottles of water, and a lot of nervous people. They should call it the sweat lodge, if you ask me.

Every few minutes, the door would open, and the lady with the headset would call out two more names.

"Extra Creddit! Come with me! You're up next," she said this time. "Selfie Town, you're on deck!"

"How much longer?" Patti asked.

"I wish I knew," I said.

So far, four bands had gone and eight of us were

still waiting. We were supposed to sit quietly, so it was just tick, tick, tick, tick, tick on the clock, until suddenly—

"Excuse me? Are you We Stink?" someone asked.

I jumped up, but it wasn't the headset lady. It was some guy with a messenger bag and a T-shirt that said "Spee-Dee Delivery."

"Yes, we stink!" I said. "I mean, we *are* We Stink."

"This is for you," he said, and gave me a big envelope addressed to the band.

"What is it?" Mari asked.

"I don't know," I said.

I'd never gotten a special delivery before. My hands shook when I ripped open the package.

Four smaller envelopes fell out. They were a pretty shade of lavender, with our names on them in fancy calligraphy. They also all said, "Open me just before you go on! Good luck!"

"Ooh, maybe it's a present from Lulu!" Nanci said.

And I thought, *maybe it's from Sam*. That would be just like him. He was so thoughtful that way.

Then the green room door opened and the stage manager called out again.

"Selfie Town, come with me, please! We Stink, you're on deck!"

My breakfast did one more triple-twisting flip in my stomach. This was the moment we'd been waiting for.

"We'd better open these now!" Mari said, and we all tore into our envelopes at the same time.

Nanci pulled out some papers. So did Mari and Patti. But when I looked in my envelope, it was empty. There was nothing inside. Just the faint smell of strawberries.

Although, not exactly, I thought. It smelled more like...Strawberry Split Lip Bomb Lip Balm.

Missy's favorite flavor.

"Wait!" I yelled at the girls. "Don't read those!"

But it was too late. They were already looking at their papers. And not in a happy, smiley kind of way.

"You think I can't sing?" Patti said.

"You think I'm too insecure?" Mari said.

"YOU THINK I TALK TOO LOUD?" Nanci said, waving her pages in my face.

That's when I got a glimpse of what they'd been reading. It looked like pages out of my journal—but it wasn't my journal. And it looked like my handwriting—but it wasn't my handwriting.

And I knew right then that I hadn't done nearly enough to get away from Missy Trillin and her wrath. Because guess what?

Rock stars and evil princesses have one thing in common: they never take the weekend off.

CHAPTER 53

Peace, Love, and Misunderstanding

How could you do this?" Mari said.

"I didn't!" I said. "Missy did. Those are obviously fake!" With all that tutoring, she'd definitely gotten plenty of samples of my handwriting.

"If this is fake, how did Missy know I liked Kyle Berg?" Patti said, waving more pages around.

"Or about my embarrassing birthmark?" Mari whispered. "It's all here."

All of a sudden, I was thinking about our We Stink band meetings in the bathroom at school. And how we never did check the stalls. And how much I was wishing we had.

"Don't you see? This is exactly what Missy wanted!" I said. "I was going to warn you, but I didn't want you to freak out before the finals—"

"Too late for that," Mari said.

"This isn't the first time you've lied to us, Georgia," Nanci said.

"I wasn't lying!" I said. "I was just—"

"Hang on. There's more here," Mari said, still reading. Then she looked right at Patti. "You told Georgia I wasn't pulling my weight? Why would you say that?"

"I didn't!" Patti said, and then she looked right at me. "Why would you write that, Georgia?"

"I DIDN'T! AREN'T YOU LISTENING TO ME?" I said, right before the stage manager opened the green room door again.

"Okay, We Stink, you're up! Come with me, please. Lila and the Carry-Ons, you're on deck!"

I couldn't believe it. Everything had come down to this—one big, fiery ball of disaster at the exact wrong moment. The timing could not have been worse.

Somewhere, Missy Trillin was looking into her magic witch's mirror and laughing her butt off.

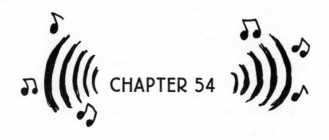

CHAPTER 54

Shake It Up

Five horrible minutes later, we were up on stage, plugged in and waiting to go. The theater was too dark to see anyone, and my mind was running like cuh-razy.

There hadn't been a chance to say anything else, and all I could think now was that I'd told them the truth. Those pages weren't mine.

What more could I do?

"Okay, next up we have..." Mr. Swivel's voice came over a microphone. "We Stink? Interesting name. Whenever you're ready, girls."

A spotlight hit me in the eyes. I took a deep breath. And Nanci counted us off.

"One! Two! One-two-three-four!"

I tried to focus during the intro. Still, you could feel the tension all over the stage. Nobody was looking at me, and the music was...

Well, actually, the music was *thumping*. In a good way. It felt kind of angry, and loud, and really rock-and-roll-y.

I just wished the girls had believed me. I was telling the truth. Those pages weren't mine.

And I couldn't get that thought out of my head. *FOCUS, GEORGIA!*

Mari was glaring at me now, and I realized I was about to miss my cue. So I stepped up to the mic just in time and blurted out the first line.

Sort of. Because what I sang was—

"I told you the truth. Those words weren't mine!" Oh. My. *OOPS!*

The girls all looked at me, completely stunned. Patti didn't have any time to react, either. Her line was next. But then she shocked me right back when she sang—

"Yeah right, don't try, 'cause we all think you're lyin'!"

I went with it.

"I'm telling you now, it's all just fake!" I sang, and Nanci brought it home.

"Yeah, right, you liar," she sang, and I saw her eyes get big. She knew what to do. "Just watch my head shake!"

And we all sang—

"Shake it, shake it, shake-a-shake-a-shake it, let's shake on it!"

It was like a rock-and-roll miracle. Just like that, we were right back in it. I don't think the audience even knew the song was supposed to go another way.

I'm not saying I'm glad we got into that fight, but I'll tell you something else. The madder we got, the better the music got. And for the first time in my life, I wasn't just pretending to be a rock star.

I actually felt like one.

CHAPTER 55

And the Winner Is...

All of the Hills Village people cheered like crazy when we finished. The judges just scribbled something on their pads. Mr. Swivel said, "Thank you!" into his mic, and that was it.

I felt GREAT. It was like all the drama had just been erased and we were right back on track. Whether or not we won, the girls and I had just pulled off something amazing. So I turned to Mari, held up my hand for a high five...

And she just walked away from me, right off the stage. Patti and Nanci were right behind her, leaving me standing there with my hand in the air and my face getting redder by the second.

So much for erasing all the drama, I guess.

Afterward, in the green room, it was so quiet you would have thought someone had pressed the Mute button. As far as I could tell, Mari was mad at Patti, Nanci was mad at Mari, everyone was mad at me, and nobody was talking to anyone. I didn't even know if We Stink had just broken up, or what.

Which was too bad, because we'd just played the best show of our lives.

After all the bands performed, they finally brought all of us back out onstage for the results. We stood there in a big line while Mr. Swivel got up in front of the families again.

"Well, well, well, isn't this exciting?" he said, and you could just feel all the kids onstage grinding their teeth down to little nubs, waiting to hear who had won.

I still wanted this. I wanted it so bad. Then maybe we could start to put the whole stupid fight behind us and just keep going.

"And our winner today—"

I mean, I could live with not winning if I had to. I just didn't want to have to.

"—is a band that showed the musical chops to stand toe-to-toe with the one and only Lulu and the Handbags—"

"JUST SAY IT!" someone yelled in the audience, and everyone laughed. Mr. Swivel kept going.

"As hard as this decision was, it was also unanimous," he said. "So, without further delay, the winning band is…"

I swallowed hard. It felt like choking down a rock.

No pun intended.

"Extra Creddit!"

A big spotlight came on and Extra Creddit was high-fiving and jumping around, while the rest of us stood around like a giant pile of leftovers.

And just like that…it was all over.

Truthfully, I never thought we'd get as far as we did. But once that happened, I wanted to hear Jordy Swivel say "WE STINK IS THE WINNER!" as much as I've ever wanted anything. Now, the girls and I were just standing there with nothing to say.

And I was starting to think that We Stink—one of the best things to ever happen to me—was no more.

If the Lulu show hadn't been that night, I would have asked Mom to sneak me out of the theater in a suitcase and get me home ASAP.

But no way. Not after everything else. I was going to stick around and meet Lulu, even if it killed me.

Which it practically did.

You'll see.

And Then This Happened

The concert was amazing times infinity. Lulu was everything I wanted her to be. Heck, she was everything *I* wanted to be. It didn't even seem real that I was going to actually meet her, until we were finally allowed to line up after the show.

I ran down the aisle to be first. Rafe was right there with his camera and Mom was getting the car so we could make a quick getaway after this. I just couldn't face the girls. I'd have to work it out with them later. *Somehow.*

They set Lulu up at a table on the stage, and we were supposed to come up, one by one, get an autograph, take a picture, and then maybe die of happiness.

"Okay, let's get rolling!" the stage manager said, and pointed at me. "You're up first, young lady."

And then I was climbing the stairs.

And then I was ON STAGE. WITH LULU.

AND LULU WAS TALKING TO ME.

I mean, her mouth was moving, but all I could hear was the sound of happy fireworks exploding in my brain.

"Hello?" Lulu said, and waved a hand in my face.

"Sorry!" I kind of gasped out. I felt like a horse had just sat on my lungs. But not in a bad way.

"You want me to sign that T-shirt, hon?" Lulu asked.

I gave her the shirt while time stood still.

"And now a picture," the stage manager said. "Do you have a camera?"

I'd forgotten to borrow Mom's phone, but Rafe was still there.

"I've got this," he said.

They let me come around behind the table so we could pose in front of the drums and amps and everything. And by *everything,* I mean Lulu. She was right there, touching me. And even breathing on me. It was the best moment of my life.

"Say 'rock and roll!'" Rafe said.

"Rock and roll!" Lulu said.

And—click!

"Thanks for coming," Lulu said. "Rock on, sister!"

I sort of laughed and sort of grunted. I didn't even realize I was backing up. It was like Lulu was the sun and I couldn't stay too close or I'd burst into flames.

"Thank *you*," I said. "I, uh...love your music... and..."

"Watch out!" she said.

"You, too!" I said—right before I backed into Brandy Venner's twenty-piece drum kit.

Correction: Right before I *fell* into Brandy Venner's drum kit, knocked over the snare, stumbled into the stool, fell backward onto the floor, and brought down a whole set of cymbals and woodblocks, right on top of myself.

OMG.

It all made this giant, banging, clanging car-crash sound while I hit the dirt like a piece of rock-and-roll roadkill.

I screamed.

Lulu screamed.

And that made everyone—and I mean *everyone*—stop and stare at me sprawled out with my thrift-shop skirt around my head.

And just in case you're wondering—no, it's not possible to make yourself disappear through the floor no matter *how* much you wish for it.

The stunned silence was finally broken when Rafe shouted, "Georgia!"

"You okay, sweetheart?" Lulu asked.

"I can't believe this," the stage manager said as she pulled me out of the wreckage.

"I'm fine," I muttered, pulling my skirt back down where it belonged.

"She's okay, she's okay!" Lulu was saying.

A lot of the other kids were laughing, or trying not to. Some of them clapped. And Rafe was pushing his way toward me.

"Georgia! Georgia!" he yelled again. When I looked, he had his camera pointed right at me. "What are you thinking about, right now—?"

GET THAT CAMERA OUT OF MY FACE!!

I probably don't have to tell you that I didn't stick around after that. I hit the stairs, ran up the aisle, and kept going.

The last thing I heard was Lulu, still back on the stage.

"Now that, ladies and gentlemen," she said, "is what you call rock and roll!"

CHAPTER 57

Virally Yours

Do you remember at the beginning of this book when I told you I got famous? Well, this might not have seemed like the time for that to happen, but it was.

I was literally an overnight sensation.

I didn't find out about it until noon the next day. And even then, I only woke up because Rafe was pounding on the door.

"Georgia!"

"What do you want?" I asked.

I felt like a piece of gum stuck to the sidewalk. The last thing I wanted to do was peel myself out of bed. Much less see anyone.

But Rafe barged in anyway. "Where's your computer?" he asked.

You can probably guess where this is going, right? My brother had posted his video of me falling into Lulu's drums, and let's just say that it was WAY more popular than We Stink.

By the time I found "Clumsy Girl Wrecks Lulu's Drums" on YouTube, it had a lot of views.

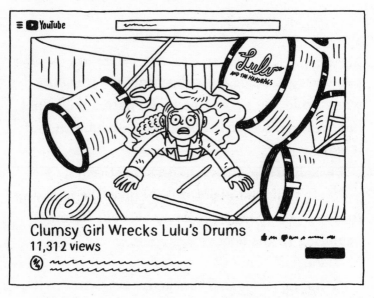

Clumsy Girl Wrecks Lulu's Drums
11,312 views

"I took mine down when I saw what was happening," Rafe said, "but by then, it kind of had a life of its own—"

"Just…stop talking," I told him.

Because there was more. Lots more.

I did a search for "Clumsy Girl Lulu Drums" and got back *hundreds* of results. Some of them were just copies of Rafe's video, but there was also one with meowing sounds for no good reason, a bunch of slow-motion versions, and at least two videos with a big fart noise added in when I fell.

"On the bright side, you're kind of famous," Rafe said. "I mean, eleven thousand hits—"

"GET OUT!" I hollered. And for once, my brother knew what was good for him. He left me alone after that.

I couldn't believe this was happening. And in fact, "Clumsy Girl" was just getting started. My video was like one of those snowballs rolling down a ski slope, getting bigger and bigger by the second. Because guess what?

Eleven thousand hits was *nothing*.

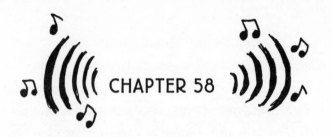

CHAPTER 58

Five Days Later...

In case you can't tell, I spent a lot of time in my room that week. And a lot of that time, I was writing.

I didn't know if it was poetry or songs or what. Not that I had a band to make songs with anymore. But Mom said I didn't have to know what it was, and to just keep writing what I felt.

What I *felt* like was shipping myself off to Bolivia in a Georgia-sized container. But that wasn't going to happen.

Meanwhile, the phone was ringing off the hook.

I got invited back to *Hills Village This Week with Marty Gruber*. Another TV show in the city wanted me to come in and re-create my big fall in their studio. And I heard from Carly Morehead at Channel 12, who wanted to "profile Clumsy Girl, up close and personal" for the weekend news.

No, no, no, no, no.

So, yeah, I was famous, all right. It was like I'd gotten exactly what I'd been wishing for.

Just without any of the good parts...and all of the bad.

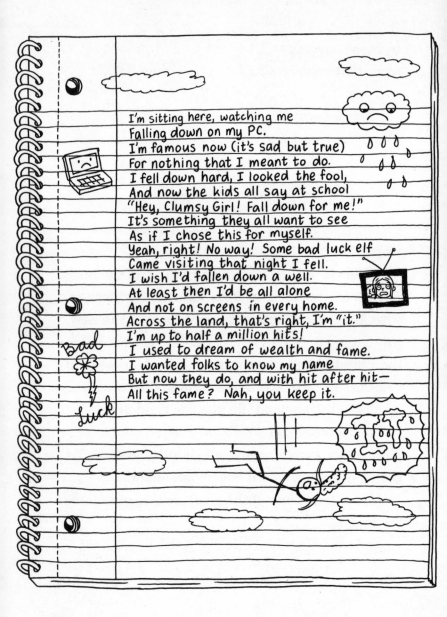

I'm sitting here, watching me
Falling down on my PC.
I'm famous now (it's sad but true)
For nothing that I meant to do.
I fell down hard, I looked the fool,
And now the kids all say at school
"Hey, Clumsy Girl! Fall down for me!"
It's something they all want to see
As if I chose this for myself.
Yeah, right! No way! Some bad luck elf
Came visiting that night I fell.
I wish I'd fallen down a well.
At least then I'd be all alone
And not on screens in every home.
Across the land, that's right, I'm "it."
I'm up to half a million hits!
I used to dream of wealth and fame.
I wanted folks to know my name
But now they do, and with hit after hit—
All this fame? Nah, you keep it.

Bad
Luck

CHAPTER 59

Sweet and Sour

After five days of the whole Clumsy Girl disaster, I felt like I had this giant We Stink–shaped hole in my life.

I missed Mari, Nanci, and Patti.

But even more than that, I missed We Stink. I missed being part of a band.

That afternoon, I went down to the studio to be alone and practice my guitar—but it didn't feel like a studio anymore. Now it was just the garage again. So I sat there, trying to play but mostly just trying not to cry.

And then I heard a familiar voice.

"How's it going in here?" Sam asked. I hadn't

even heard him come in, but I stopped playing as soon as I saw him.

"Don't stop," he said. "It sounded good. Oh, and I brought you these."

He handed me a pack of Skittles—the extra-sour kind. Those were my favorite, which was super-sweet of him. But when I tried to eat one, the giant lump in my throat got in the way.

"I don't want to cry in front of you," I said. "I'm so embarrassed. About all of it."

"It's okay if you do," he said. "I don't mind."

And even though I still didn't want to cry, I couldn't help it.

"I know I should try to focus on the positive," I said. "That's what Mom always tells me."

"That's good advice," Sam said. "But sometimes you need to be sad for a while first."

I just kind of looked at him then, with my eyes all red and puffy. I knew Sam was smart in school, but I didn't know he was smart about this stuff, too. It helped, some. I even managed to share those Skittles with him after a little while.

So it wasn't all bad.

Just *mostly* bad.

CHAPTER 60

But Then...

Georgia!" Mom said, knocking on my door that night. "There's someone on the phone for you."

"Is it Sam?" I asked.

"No," Mom said.

"Then no thanks," I said.

She opened my door anyway and held out the phone. "It's from the mayor's office," she said. "I think you're going to want to take this one."

I wasn't so sure. What now? Did they want Clumsy Girl to fall off a Fourth of July parade float or something?

"Hello?" I said.

"Hi Georgia, my name is Britt and I'm calling

from the Hills Village Arts Council," she said. "I saw your video online—"

"I'm not interested," I said.

"Excuse me?" she said.

"Clumsy Girl has no comment," I said.

"Sorry. I don't know what you're talking about," the woman told me. "I'm calling about the We Stink Rock-You-Mentary, but maybe I have the wrong number."

And that's when everything started to change again.

CHAPTER 61

Not Exactly Over

So what do you want from us, Georgia?" Patti asked.

I'd basically forced the girls to come over to the studio. We Stink hadn't practiced in a week, and maybe didn't exist anymore.

I didn't know how long I could keep them there, so I got right to it.

"We've been invited to perform at City Hall," I said.

"Again?" Mari said.

"Not in the park. Legitimately. Inside the main auditorium," I said. "And they want to show Rafe's movie, too."

I'd stopped calling it "our" movie. The whole time I'd been hibernating in my room, Rafe was in his room, editing that thing like a mad video scientist and getting it posted online everywhere. I knew he felt bad about what had happened, and besides, I just didn't have the energy to kill him anymore. In fact, I was actually pretty grateful for his help, despite how it all went down in the end.

"I don't know, Georgia," Nanci said. "I'll come to the movie, but I don't want to perform."

"Yeah," Patti said, and Mari nodded.

"I understand," I said.

And I did. This was my own fault. I should have trusted the girls before the finals and told them the truth right away. But *noooooo,* I had to go and turn a really good thing into a big sloppy mess instead. I tried to solve all of our problems on my own, but we were a band—a team. And now I know what happens when you try to solve things alone.

Disaster.

They'd already accepted my apology, but only in that way where it was still kind of weird and cold between all of us.

"No offense, Georgia," Patti said. "I guess maybe We Stink should just take a break for a while."

I didn't point out the obvious part. We Stink already *was* taking a break. And I've seen enough romantic comedies to know what that really meant. *Taking a break* always comes right before the saddest part of the movie.

But I didn't push it. I said I'd just meet them

at City Hall on the night of the screening. And everyone said okay, even though it seemed like we weren't even friends anymore.

But I wasn't giving up, either. If you haven't noticed yet, I don't give up. I'm a Khatchadorian.

I still had at least one more idea.

So I went back to my room, closed the door, and kept on writing.

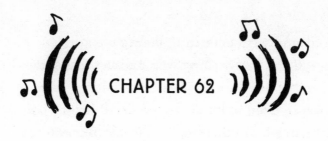

Four of Hearts

City Hall auditorium was almost full on the night we showed the movie. A whole bunch of people were there, including Jeanne Galletta, Flip, and, of course, Sam. But also people I didn't even know—from school and from around Hills Village.

Now that Clumsy Girl was "famous," people actually wanted to know more about the band. And they wanted to see the Rock-You-Mentary, too.

Mari, Nanci, and Patti all sat in different places in the auditorium. I had to stand up in front and say something before we started.

And the funny thing was, I didn't feel super-scared or nervous. I guess I was getting used to being in front of an audience. Or at least I had been, until our band dissolved into a puddle of disaster.

"Hi, everyone," I said. "Thanks for coming. We Stink is really proud of our Rock-You-Mentary and can't wait for you to see it. We're going to show the movie in just a minute, but I want to do one quick thing first."

Sam came over and set a stool down onstage and handed me my guitar. Rafe brought down the lights from the back. And then I started to play.

"This is for Mari, Patti, and Nanci," I said. "They'll know why."

I hadn't memorized the words to the song yet. It was still brand-new. So I had a cheat sheet on the floor in front of me, just in case.

But you know what? I didn't need it.

Because this song came straight from the heart.

Four of Hearts

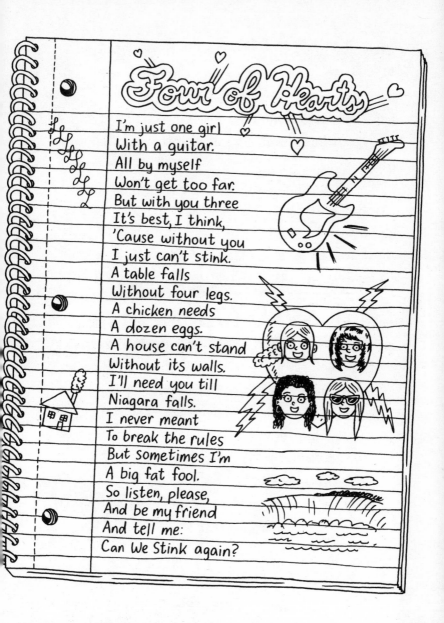

I'm just one girl
With a guitar.
All by myself
Won't get too far.
But with you three
It's best, I think,
'Cause without you
I just can't stink.
A table falls
Without four legs.
A chicken needs
A dozen eggs.
A house can't stand
Without its walls.
I'll need you till
Niagara falls.
I never meant
To break the rules
But sometimes I'm
A big fat fool.
So listen, please,
And be my friend
And tell me:
Can We Stink again?

CHAPTER 63

We Stink

A ROCK-YOU-MENTARY

by Rafe Khatchadorian

40) Asfkgdql
41) We Stink
42) The Backpacks
43) Selfie-Powered

KEEP THOSE VOTES COMING IN!

THE END

*Dedicated to Flip Savage,
who took one for the team*

Special thanks to Jeanne Galletta and Sam Marks

Togetherness

The girls and I all hugged it out that night, and we even all stayed over at Mari's. It turned out they all missed the band as much as I did, but nobody wanted to be the first one to say it. I guess we were all just suddenly afraid of being honest with each other. And you can't be dishonest with your best friends. Which was just one more reason why I wasn't going to keep anything from them anymore.

And just to prove it, I let them read my whole journal. There wasn't anything about them in there, anyway. Just a bunch of really bad song ideas, and a couple of really good ones. And a whole lot of really weird doodles.

Which brings me to what happened next.

Mom says some guy named Andy Warhol once said that in the future, everyone will be famous for fifteen minutes. And even though Clumsy Girl lasted longer than that, she did go away after a while. Especially after some kid lost his pants when he fell into the monkey enclosure at the San Diego Zoo and racked up about a zillion hits. Poor kid. I know how he feels.

Meanwhile, now that Clumsy Girl and the Rock-You-Mentary had paved the way, We Stink was getting a whole bunch of new followers. And new requests, too.

We played at school again, and at the mall, and at Mari's dad's used car lot, and a whole bunch of birthday parties, too. We played new music, old music, and even learned some classic rock covers. We called the whole thing WE STINK: THE REUNION TOUR.

And it's still going strong.

By the Way

You're probably wondering what happened to Missy. That one's kind of complicated. We didn't call a truce or anything. It was more like...well, let's just say we're taking a break.

Should I have apologized to her for what I did? Yes and no, if you ask me. And that's where I was stuck.

I couldn't get Missy her phone back, but she couldn't get us another shot with Lulu, either.

And I don't think Missy saw it coming when I told her what *really* happened at the finals.

"If it wasn't for you, we wouldn't have given the best performance of our lives," I said.

"I'm getting uncomfortable now," Missy said.

"Don't worry, I'm not going to thank you," I told her.

"Good," she said, and we left it at that.

Will Missy and I ever get back together again? And by *get back together*, I mean will we go back to making each other's life miserable?

Maybe.

Well, probably.

Okay, almost definitely.

But in the meantime, I'm not going out of my way to pick any fights. In fact, I'm going to try to be more like Sam. He doesn't care about the Princesses either way. Maybe that makes him a geek in their eyes, but I think it's one of the coolest things about him.

And speaking of Sam...

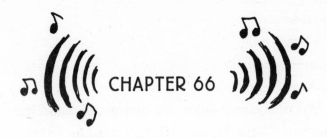

Onward and Upward

When Mrs. Hibbs told Sam and me to stay after class, I thought it was because we'd been talking too much during her lecture.

But it wasn't anything like that.

"There's a regional competition for Rube Goldberg machines in Chicago this summer," she said. "I thought you two might be interested."

"What do we have to do?" Sam asked.

"Just build the best, most innovative machine you can think of," she said. "After that, the winners go on to the nationals in Washington, DC. But let's focus on one step at a time."

Sam looked at me like, *Are you thinking what I'm thinking?* And I looked back at him like, *I think I am.*

Then we both blurted it out at the same time. Except he said, "Windmill power!" And I said, "All the way to nationals!"

"Well, it sounds like you both bring something to the table." Mrs. Hibbs said. "Now, if I could just get you to stop talking during class…"

We took a brochure to show our parents. And then out in the hall, we stopped by my locker to talk about it some more.

"This is going to take a lot of work," Sam said. "What about your band?"

"We're good," I said. "Once school's out, we'll have plenty of time for practicing and gigs."

"Very cool," Sam said. "So I guess we're doing this."

"I guess we are," I said, and we even shook on it.

Then we looked around to make sure Mrs. Stricker wasn't nearby, and we kissed on it, too. (Don't tell.)

We've got big plans now. And Mrs. Hibbs is right. Sam and I make a great team. This machine is going to be beyond awesome.

So watch out, Chicago, and watch out, world, because here I come!

Again.

Read on for a sneak peek at the next hilarious
book in the Middle School series

MASTER OF DISASTER

DEEP SPACE,
DEEPER TROUBLE

First of all, let me tell you that everything in this story really happened. It's just that some of it happened in my real life, and some of it happened in my imagination.

Don't say I didn't warn you.

So there I am one day, speeding along the edge of the galaxy in my one-man FTL cruiser. I've got the thrusters maxed out, way past the speed of light, and I'm passing planets, wormholes, supernovas, and space trash like they're snails along the highway.

No big deal. Just an average Tuesday afternoon in deep space…right up until my navigation alert system lights up like an intergalactic Christmas tree.

"Warning!" says a robotic voice. "You are approaching a hostile alien craft. Impact at current velocity will occur in six point two seconds."

It's not just any hostile sector, either. I've stumbled into the Stricker Quadrant, the most dangerous neighborhood in the known universe. I should have been paying closer attention. That'll teach me to eat chips and salsa while I'm jetting at 1.843 times the speed of light.

With a flick of my thumb, I reverse all thrusters. I cut the engines as fast as I can. But it's not fast enough. All it does is slow me down just before—*SKRA-PLAM!*—I crash straight into the mother of all mother ships.

I'm dazed. I'm confused. I try to scramble into my survival pod so I can jettison myself to safety, but there's no time for that. A huge robotic claw sweeps out from the side of the mother ship and pries open my cruiser like a can of tuna fish.

"WHAT IN THE WORLD DO YOU THINK YOU'RE DOING?" a voice booms out, as the claw reaches again and grabs me by the collar of my space suit.

And that's when I know for sure that I've just flown my last mission.

DEALER'S CHOICE

Rafe? I asked you a question! What in the world do you think you're doing?!"

I shook my head to clear my thoughts. I blinked a couple of times.

And I realized, of course, that I wasn't in the outer reaches of space. It was just an out-of-the-way hallway at my school.

And I hadn't been piloting a spaceship at all. It was just my new skateboard. I'd been itching *all day* to try it out on the super-smooth hallways after school let out.

And even though I hadn't just been nabbed by a hostile alien species, I *was* in danger. Big-time. Because I'd just crashed my board right into the last person on earth you'd want to do that to.

Also known as my principal, Mrs. Stricker.

"On second thought," Mrs. Stricker said, "I don't *care* what you think you're doing. Just march!"

Less than a minute later, I was back in the principal's office—again—and waiting for my latest punishment—again.

I don't want to brag, but if Hills Village Middle School had a Detention Hall of Fame, they'd practically have to name it after me. So I was pretty sure about what was coming next.

But I was wrong, wrong, wrong.

"Rafe, today just might be your lucky day," Mrs. Stricker told me. "Normally, I'd give you at least five detentions for a stunt like that. However, I want to offer you a deal."

"Excuse me?" I said.

The thing is, Mrs. Stricker doesn't *do* deals. Not unless "buy one detention, get ten free" counts. "It sounded like you just said you wanted to offer me a deal," I told her. "But that can't be right."

"You heard me correctly," Mrs. Stricker said. "We're in a rare moment where you actually might be of assistance to me, for once in your life. Extraordinary, I know. Here is your choice: you can either report to detention every Tuesday for the next five weeks, or—"

"I'll take the other thing," I said.

It didn't matter what it was. If I got another month's worth of detention, my brain was going to shrivel up and die of boredom. Seriously.

"Very well," she said, and got up to go. "Follow me."

"Where are we going?" I asked.

"Across the street to the elementary school," she said. And I thought, *Did I just get myself sent back to fifth grade?* Maybe Mrs. Stricker was so sick of me, she was sending me back to my old school.

But it wasn't that, either.

"Mrs. Melindez broke her leg slipping on a ketchup spill in the cafeteria today," Mrs. Stricker said. "I've been asked to find a substitute teacher for the after-school art program. That's going to be you."

"Seriously?" I said. "I can't believe you want me to teach *anything*."

"I don't," she said. "But I am in a bit of a pinch at this late hour."

"Wow," I said. "That must be *some* pinch!"

I mean, I know something about art. It's my best subject in school. Actually, it's my only good subject in school. But still, I'm about as far from being a *teacher* as you can get. I'm more like the kid who makes teachers wish they'd chosen some other profession.

Not that I was arguing. I mean, one hour of teaching art to little kids, in exchange for five hours of detention? That *was* a good deal.

Besides, it was too late to turn back now.

Operation: Nuclear Sub(stitute Teacher) was under way.

ROUGH LANDING

You will stick to the basics. Paint, drawing, or clay," Mrs. Stricker said while we walked, double time, over to the elementary school. "You will give the students an assignment they can take home at the end of the hour. And you will behave responsibly, or you *will* be sent back to detention. Have you got that?"

"Got it," I said.

"Good, because here we are," she said.

We were standing outside a closed classroom door now. On the other side, it sounded like someone was moving furniture. And breaking things.

And I heard yelling, too. Lots and lots of yelling.

"What's all that noise?" I asked.

"That," she told me, "is your class."

"But how—"

"Good luck," she said. I had a feeling the rest of that sentence was something like "because you're going to need it." But Mrs. Stricker didn't stick around long enough for me to find out.

So I reached out, opened the art-room door, and—

FWOOM!

It was like getting punched in the face. By a tornado. Made of third graders.

"Okay, you guys!" I called out. "Everyone come over here, sit down, and listen up."

I'll give you four guesses for what happened after that:

(A) Everyone came over here

(B) Everyone sat down

(C) Everyone listened up

(D) None of the above

If you guessed (D), you win. Meanwhile, I hadn't even started and I was already losing. I could just smell those detentions getting closer.

So what do I do next? I move on to Plan B, of course. I reach out and push the big red button on the wall. The one marked SCHOOL-BOT 2000 AUTOMATED SYSTEM. USE ONLY IN EMERGENCIES.

Then I let the automated system do the rest.

A secret panel slides open in the ceiling. Twelve metal Frisbees with embedded homing devices fly out and hover in the air next to me, waiting for their next command.

"Fetch!" I tell them. And just like that, they

move in on their targets, each one attaching itself to the butt of a different kid.

"SYSTEM ENGAGED!" the system tells me. Which means I'm ready for Plan B, Phase Two.

"What's going on?" a little kid asks.

"I can't get this thing off me!" another says.

"Proceed to Phase Two!" I tell the system.

A loud humming noise fills the air as the electric magnets in the art-room seats buzz to life.

"Hey!" another kid says, as he's pulled across the room by the back of his pants.

"What's happening?" another asks, just before—*CLUNK!*—his metallized rear end attaches to the magnets in his chair. Followed by eleven others.

CLUMP!

CLANK!

CLOMP!

BUMP!

ZZT!

BANG!

FWIP!

SHLIP!

BLORNG!

FWANK!

TRANK!

And just like that, I've taken control of my class. Not bad for a first-time substitute, huh?

The only problem being, of course, that I wasn't so lucky. But you already knew that, didn't you?

In fact, I was still just standing there, wondering how to get twelve little kids to sit down, make some art, and keep me from landing in middle-school prison every Tuesday for the next five weeks. Which meant it was time for the *real* Plan B.

So I did what older brothers have done for all of eternity, whenever they need to get something done.

"HEY!" I yelled in my big-brother-est voice. "EVERYONE PIPE DOWN AND FIND A SEAT OR I'M NOT GOING TO BE HELD RESPONSIBLE FOR WHAT HAPPENS NEXT!"

That used to work on my little sister, Georgia, every time. It doesn't anymore, but it sure got these kids' attention. They all stopped and stared at me like I actually meant what I said. And after that, everything went just *great*.

For about another twenty seconds.

LET'S TRY THAT AGAiN

 Now that I had their attention, I passed out paper, paints, and paintbrushes to get the kids going. Maybe this wasn't going to be so hard after all.

"Okay, guys, here's what you're going to do," I said. "I want you to paint a picture of your house."

"That's SO boring!" one kid said.

"I hate painting!" another kid said.

"Can I paint something else?" someone asked.

"No," I said. "That's the assignment, and that's that."

I really did sound like a teacher now, which was kind of depressing. But I couldn't afford to mess around.

"Any questions?" I asked, and one girl's hand shot up. "What's your name?"

"Melinda," she said.

"Thanks for raising your hand, Melinda," I said. "And what's your question?"

"Where's Jake?" she asked.

"Who?" I asked.

"Jake," another kid said. "You know. *Jake.*"

I still didn't know which one was Jake, so I did a quick head count of my twelve students and came up with…eleven heads.

"Did anyone see Jake?" I asked, and all eleven hands went up. "Great! And who saw where he went?" All eleven hands went back down.

Oh, man! I didn't know how many detentions I might get for losing an actual kid, but something told me it was more than five.

Okay, Khatchadorian, I thought. *Don't panic. You've got this.*

"Everyone just wait here," I said. Right before I realized that probably wasn't a good idea.

"Actually, everyone come with me," I said. Right before I realized that wasn't such a good idea either. The second we left that room, all eleven of them were going to spin off in eleven different directions.

So I thought of something else.

"Change of plans," I said. "Everyone give me your shoelaces."

"What for?" Melinda asked.

"The faster you give me your shoelaces, the sooner you'll find out," I said.

It took a few more minutes after that, but pretty soon, I was ready to go.

"All right, people, let's move out," I told them. "Keep your eyes peeled and your minds sharp. Operation: Find Jake At All Costs is a go!"

HiDe AND SeeK
(AND SeeK, AND SeeK)

We turned that school upside down. We went up the hall, shouting for Jake and looking in every open room. We checked the boys' bathrooms. We checked the girls' bathrooms. We checked the music room, the auditorium, the gym, the locker rooms, and the underside of all the buses in the parking lot.

No Jake.

Nope. Not under here, either.

HILLS VILLAGE MIDDLE SCHOOL

By the time we headed back to the art room, it was 4:15 and I had exactly fifteen minutes to find Jake and get the kids to make some art before the parents showed up. Either that, or leave town and never show my face in Hills Village again.

But then it turned out that I didn't have to decide. Because when we got back, there was Jake, sitting at one of the tables.

"Where have you guys been?" he asked.

"Where have *we* been?" I asked. *"Where were you?"*

He pointed down, under his table. "Taking a nap," he said. "We had subtraction today, and math makes me really sleepy."

And while I could relate to the math part, I didn't have time to be mad. I now had *fourteen* minutes left, and the kids were already getting crazy again. I had to yank one of them off the windowsill just before she could climb outside.

And that's when it hit me. These kids were like twelve of *me*. Twelve little Rafes, running around like crazy, getting into trouble, and just about impossible to focus.

So I needed something to get their attention.

Something that would have gotten *my* attention when I was their age.

And then my brain went *STORM!* And I knew what we were going to do.

Cloudy with a chance of brainstorms.

"Okay, guys," I told them. "We don't have much time, so I have a new idea. I want you all to paint me instead."

"BORING!" said the same kid as the last time.

"That's even more boring than painting a house!" Melinda said.

"No, it's not," I said. "See, I don't think you're getting my drift. Let me try that again...."

MASTERPIECE...ISH

For the rest of the hour, the kids *really* got into the assignment. I didn't have to *make* them do anything at all. They tackled this one like it was chocolate cake.

By the time the parents got there, our group project was done. It was a masterpiece! Well, close enough, anyway.

And all the kids wanted to get their picture taken next to their new creation so they could print out the photo at home and put it up on their refrigerators.

Because they'd done exactly what I'd told them to do.

They'd painted *me*.

When Mrs. Stricker came in to see how everything had gone, she looked like she was going to self-destruct.

"What in the WORLD…?" she started to say, just before Melinda's mom interrupted.

"Mrs. Stricker, I don't know what you told this young man, but I've never seen my daughter more excited about art!!" she said. "I certainly hope he'll be teaching the rest of your art program!"

The other kids were nodding. The parents were smiling. And Mrs. Stricker looked like Melinda's mom had just been speaking Martian.

"I, uh…well…uh…." she said. "The original teacher *is* going to be out for a while with a broken leg. So…I suppose that's up to Rafe."

And since something told me I was going to need to cash in some of my other detentions (the ones I hadn't gotten yet), and also because I ended up having a blast with those crazy kids (believe it or not), I said that sounded like a good idea to me.

So who knows? Maybe I have a whole career as an art teacher ahead of me. Or maybe I just got lucky that day. All I know for sure is that sometimes, a little imagination can go a long way.

And a lot of imagination can go even further.

GET YOUR PAWS ON THE

HILARIOUS DOG DIARIES SERIES!

Read the Middle School series

Visit the **Middle School world** on the Penguin website
to find out more! **www.penguin.co.uk**

THE
MIDDLE
SCHOOL
SERIES

THE WORST YEARS OF MY LIFE
(with Chris Tebbetts)

This is the insane story of my first year at middle school, when I, Rafe Khatchadorian, took on a real-life bear (sort of), sold my soul to the school bully, and fell for the most popular girl in school. Come join me, if you dare . . .

GET ME OUT OF HERE!
(with Chris Tebbetts)

We've moved to the big city, where I'm going to a super-fancy art school. The first project is to create something based on our exciting lives. But my life is TOTALLY BORING. It's time for Operation Get a Life.

MY BROTHER IS A BiG, FAT LiAR
(with Lisa Papademetriou)

So you've heard all about my big brother, Rafe, and now it's time to set the record straight. (Almost) EVERYTHING he says is a Big, Fat Lie. I'm Georgia, and it's time for some payback . . . Khatchadorian style.

HOW I SURVIVED BULLIES, BROCCOLI, AND SNAKE HILL
(with Chris Tebbetts)

I'm excited for a fun summer at camp—until I find out it's a summer *school* camp. There's no fun and games here, just a whole lotta trouble!

ULTIMATE SHOWDOWN
(with Julia Bergen)

Who would have thought that we—Rafe and Georgia—would ever agree on anything? That's right—we're writing a book together. And the best part? We want you to be part of the fun too!

SAVE RAFE!
(with Chris Tebbetts)

I'm in worse trouble than ever! I need to survive a gut-bustingly impossible outdoor excursion so I can return to school next year. But will I get through in one piece?

JUST MY ROTTEN LUCK
(with Chris Tebbetts)

I'm heading back to Hills Village Middle School, but only if I take "special classes" . . . If that wasn't bad enough, when I somehow land a place on the school football team, I find myself playing alongside the biggest bully in school, Miller the Killer!

DOG'S BEST FRIEND
(with Chris Tebbetts)
It's a dog-eat-dog world. When I start my own dog-walking empire, I didn't think it could go so horribly wrong! Somehow, I always seem to end up in deep doo-doo . . .

ESCAPE TO AUSTRALIA
(with Martin Chatterton)
I just won an all-expenses paid trip of a lifetime to Australia. But here's the bad news: I MIGHT NOT MAKE IT OUT ALIVE!

FROM HERO TO ZERO
(with Chris Tebbetts)
I'm going on a class trip to London! What could possibly go wrong? I've spent all of middle school being chased by Miller the Killer, but on this trip, there's NOWHERE TO RUN!

ALSO BY JAMES PATTERSON

I FUNNY SERIES
I Funny (*with Chris Grabenstein*)
I Even Funnier (*with Chris Grabenstein*)
I Totally Funniest (*with Chris Grabenstein*)
I Funny TV (*with Chris Grabenstein*)
School of Laughs (*with Chris Grabenstein*)
The Nerdiest, Wimpiest, Dorkiest I Funny Ever
(*with Chris Grabenstein*)

OTHER ILLUSTRATED NOVELS

For more information about James Patterson's novels,
visit www.jamespatterson.co.uk

MALPAS
25/1/20

Community Learning & Libraries
Cymuned Ddysgu a Llyfrgelloedd

This item should be returned or renewed by the
last date stamped below.

6/6

MALPAS

JAMES PATTERSON is the bestselling author of the Middle School series, the Maximum Ride, Witch & Wizard, Daniel X and the I Funny series. He lives in Florida.

CHRIS TEBBETTS

NEIL SWAAB is a New York City-based illustrator.